Fetching the Dead

A list of books in the series appears at the end of this volume.

FETCHING THE DEAD

Stories by

Scott R. Sanders

UNIVERSITY OF ILLINOIS PRESS

Urbana and Chicago

*Publication of this work was supported in part
by grants from the National Endowment for the Arts
and the Illinois Arts Council, a state agency.*

This book is printed on acid-free paper.

Earlier versions of stories from this collection originally appeared in the
following periodicals:

"The Recovery of Vision," *North American Review* 266, no. 1 (March 1981).
"Fetching the Dead," *Stand* 12, no. 1 (Winter 1971).
"Walking to Sleep," *Carolina Quarterly* 29, no. 1 (Winter 1977).
"The Cry," *Brushfire* 25 (Spring 1976).
"Prophet," *Transatlantic Review* 33/34 (Winter 1970).
"The Fire Woman," *Cross Fertilization,* ed. Morty Sklar (Iowa City: The
Spirit That Moves Us, 1980).
"Time and Again," *Tracks* 6, no. 2 (Spring 1978); reprinted in *The Maga-
zine of Fantasy and Science Fiction* 61, no. 6 (November 1981).

Library of Congress Cataloging in Publication Data

Sanders, Scott R. (Scott Russell), 1945–
Fetching the dead.

(Illinois short fiction)
Contents: The recovery of vision — Fetching the dead — Wake — [etc.]
I. Title. II. Series.
PS3569.A5137F4   1984   813'.54   83-17668
ISBN 0-252-01115-5

To Eva Mary Solomon Sanders
with love

*I conceive that land belongs for us to a vast family
of which many are dead,
few are living,
and countless numbers
are still unborn.*

— *Nigerian tribesman*

Contents

The Recovery of Vision   1

Fetching the Dead   18

Wake   37

Walking to Sleep   56

The Cry   77

Prophet   96

The Fire Woman   111

Time and Again   127

The Recovery of Vision

While Sierra bought tickets for the bus to Edinburgh, Hazard calculated how many dulcimers he would have to make and sell in order to pay her back. And he might have to make them blind, too, if these drops failed to cure the infection in his eyes. His money had run out nine days into their fifteen-day hurricane tour of England. Now he was traveling on her charity, as he had slept and eaten on it for most of the two years they had been living together in Memphis. When she told him the ticket price, with her wry smile in place as usual, he wrote the figure on the card in his wallet where he kept a running total of his debt to her.

It was an astronomical debt, enough to make a Rockefeller weep. When they flew home to Memphis after New Year's, he would have to quit building dulcimers and fiddles and fretless banjos, lay aside that nickel-and-dime craft he loved so well, and try to weasel back into his forklift job at Firestone. Ach, the stink of rubber!

Let's break out of this two-year rut of loving indecision, she had urged him. Let's fly to England for Christmas, decide about marriage. England? he had stammered. Marriage?

Eleven frazzled days into the trip—his eyes inflamed by some germ picked up off a handrail or doorknob, his wallet empty except for the record of debts—Hazard was snarled worse than ever in loving indecision. After hustling through London, Canterbury, Oxford, and a dozen intervening curiosities; after dawn at Stonehenge; after evensong at Ely Cathedral; after darts and hard cider and a Baedecker's worth of pubs, he was convinced he would never overcome his fatigue or his debt or his fear of joining himself to this woman. Whenever he imagined marriage he saw his grandmother and grandfather on their fiftieth wedding anniversary, their hands joined to form an arch through which the twenty-seven grandchildren paraded. If either one had let go, both old people would have fallen. It was the leaning together that frightened him, as if marriage were a schooling in need.

At dusk on the eleventh day a red double-decker bus trundled them from Cambridge to Lesser Blithey, where they would catch the Edinburgh express. Hazard sagged to the pavement beneath the one streetlight in the village, his back propped against the locked door of a sweet-shop. Posters in the window advertised chocolate and tobacco and lottery tickets.

"Let's explore the great metropolis of Lesser Blithey," Sierra suggested. "We have till nearly midnight."

"I can see it all from here." And he could, too—the twin rows of cottages and the parish church, all of somber granite, flanking the London-Edinburgh highway like oversized gravestones.

"Here, then, Mister Sit-tight—have another burden." Sierra plumped her rucksack down in his lap, and then with arms outstretched like a tightrope walker's, she balanced on the curb and tiptoed out of sight beyond the circle of streetlight.

Late as it was, organ music groaned from the church. Judging from the false starts and repeated phrases, this was a rehearsal, not a performance. Did the village hobble off to sleep on these tortured melodies? Still, it couldn't touch the awfulness of a poorly-scraped fiddle. With eyes shut, Hazard listened to the organ and the whine of truck tires. Lorries, the British called them. What an odd prissy language. His eyes felt as if there were cinders beneath the lids. The pavement chilled him through his corduroy trousers and his insulated long johns. Meanwhile, Sierra was out there circling in the darkness, spinning about her own axis.

He was on the point of going to hunt for her when she came cat-footing back along the curb, her face in its parka hood catching the sheen of streetlight. She held a knobby hard roll in each gloved hand.

"Here's a little supper," she said.

"Where on earth did you find them?"

"I followed my nose to a kitchen door, knocked very politely, and bought them from a woman who had flour in her hair."

"It's a wonder she didn't shoot you."

"We're not in Tennessee, my dear vigilante."

Slapping his arms with hands that felt numb as planks, he replied, "Tennessee hasn't been this cold since the last ice age."

"Well, quit squatting there like some idiotic penguin, and let's go eat our rolls in the church."

"But there's somebody in there murdering the organ. Just listen."

"So we'll dine to music. Up, hero." She clamped one of the rolls in her teeth and pulled at his sleeve. "On your frozen feet."

Inside the huge ironclad doors of the church, the music sounded less tortured, more like the booming splash of waters on a rocky coast. Glimpsing the organist, who had a neck as thick as a stevedore's and hands like baseball gloves, Hazard balked. "He won't care," Sierra whispered, guiding him into a pew. "Not everybody's as self-conscious about his music as you are." The only light in the place glowed above the organ. There was no heat, of course, but the walls offered shelter from the north wind.

While they munched their hard rolls they soaked in the rumbling tones of the organ. Each note lit fires on the inside of Hazard's eyelids. After a thunderstorm finale, the cover slammed down over the keyboard and the organist came shuffling along the aisle with a fistful of sheet music. Spying Hazard and Sierra, he called out amiably, "Rather a sorry concert, I'm afraid."

"Practice makes perfect," Sierra answered. "Really, it was lovely."

He shrugged. Hazard imagined him shouldering halves of beef onto ships. Three layers of sweater showed at his neck. "Keeping warm?" the organist inquired.

"We're trying to," Sierra replied. "We're waiting for the eleven-fifty bus."

"Off to Edinburgh, is it? Then you must come have some tea with an old displaced Scot. It's only just next door."

They sipped jasmine tea. The organist unfolded a map of Edinburgh across his knees, and showed them with a black-nailed thumb where to visit. Sierra drew him into talk as if he were an uncle.

"Who knitted the afghan?" she asked, patting the couch-cover.

"My wife, before the Lord took her away. It's on account of her I'm learning the organ."

"She played, did she?"

"Fit for heaven, fit for heaven." The man sighed like airbrakes on a train, and Sierra rested a hand on his arm.

Hazard forgot the ache in his eyes, watching Sierra work her charm. Without her gumption to spur him on, he would still have been outside shivering on the sidewalk. In fact, he would still be hauling warm tires around the Firestone warehouse in Memphis. Quit that stupid job, she had urged him; move in with me; make your instruments on the kitchen table. After weeks of shilly-shallying, he had agreed, on the condition that he would pay back his share of rent and food when musicians started journeying from the four corners of America to buy his instruments. "So what's to pay back?" she had said then with a baffled smile. But he had insisted on keeping track of how much he owed her, remembering his father's advice that a man pays his own way and stands on his own feet. And so his tools and lumber filled one of her two bedrooms. When they made love, she would pick woodshavings from his beard.

For two years the stack of cards, with its inked trail of indebtedness, grew thicker. He sold every instrument he built — the fiddles with their tiger-maple bellies, the dulcimers with their rosewood ribs — but he could not charge enough to make a living. "We make a living between us," Sierra would say. "We both work. The hospital just happens to overpay me for managing their business, and all these skinflint musicians underpay you for your instruments." Lean on me, she seemed to be saying. That would enrage Hazard, and he would end up sleeping on cushions atop his pile of air-cured lumber, humiliated by his need for her.

"Not to hurry you," the organist was saying, "but it's half past, and the bus drivers sometimes use a heavy foot coming up from London." He sat there in his overstuffed armchair with a hand splayed over each knee, like a catcher in the dugout wearing two mitts.

Sierra patted one of those hands. "Keep at your music. We'll think of you when we're in Edinburgh."

"Do that, love. Mind you, don't forget the sunset at the castle. It's one of God's wonders. And take a look at the Walter Scott monument."

"We'll remember." Sierra bent over and kissed him on the cheek.

Hazard echoed her thanks, envying the organist for the firm way he sat in his chair.

Beneath the streetlight again, rucksacks slung over shoulders, they huddled against a wind that seemed to arrive directly from Siberia. Trucks and cars whooshed by at intervals of one or two minutes. The few lighted windows of Lesser Blithey winked out one by one.

"What we do to save the price of a bed-and-breakfast!" Sierra muttered. Hazard bristled at that, because it had been his idea to take the overnight bus to Edinburgh. She stamped her feet. "So how are the peepers?"

"They're coming along fine," Hazard lied.

"You didn't act like they were coming along any too fine back there at our friend the organist's, the way you kept them all squinted up. Stoop down here, let me see. Ugh, they look like raw hamburger."

"They're doing all right."

"Did you put in your drops while I was off gallivanting?"

"I forgot."

"Forgot! The doctor said every two hours."

"I'll do it in the bus."

"Hazard, you are the most exasperating idiot." She paced back and forth with arms crossed over her chest and hands tucked under the arms, her voice rising. "You're not a soldier, you know. Nobody's going to give you a purple heart for going blind on a trip to England."

"People are sleeping," he hissed, nodding at the darkened cottages.

"You read too many war comics as a kid. Or was it Davy Crockett movies?"

"Sierra, listen —"

"I know the scenario," she went on, assuming the portentous voice of a television narrator. "The warrior marches on through ambushes and explosions, his legs tied up in splints, bandages around his skull, a bullet clenched between his teeth —"

"Stop the lecture and *listen*."

The diesel growl was unmistakable. As the organist had predicted, it was a few minutes early. Headlights, bumper gleam, lighted rectangular destination-board on the forehead of the bus. EDINBURGH, the lighted panel read. The bus slowed down for the village—then whisked past into the night again without stopping.

Hazard spun around on the curb, fist raised, and shouted, "Hey, you son of a bitch!"

"Shush, people are sleeping!" Sierra mimicked. She was laughing as the tail-lights vanished northward. "So much for British transport."

Hazard turned on her. "You think it's funny for us to freeze out here because that fool forgot to pick us up?"

She gave him an appraising look. "Don't you think it's funny?"

The sudden calming of her voice warned him that she wanted a serious answer. It was one of her little tests, to discover how many rooms there were inside his head, to see how resilient a husband he might be. So he thought about the two of them stranded there at midnight in Lesser Blithey, the Siberian wind cutting through them, the village snoozing, the puzzle of love knotted up between them, and he knew it was absurd, hilarious. "The organist has a couch," he said at last.

"Let's go ask about it." Her smile broke over him like a spill of light.

Before they could stir, however, a second bus growled into view, with EDINBURGH emblazoned on the front—and it also roared past. They turned to watch it hustle by, like spectators at a horse race. Then a third bus whistled through, and a fourth, each one with a driver hunched over the wheel as if divining his fortune from the paint stripes on the highway. After the fifth bus, Hazard moaned, "I don't believe this."

"Maybe it's an evacuation," Sierra said giddily. "Maybe they're ferrying the whole population of London to Edinburgh."

As she spoke, a sixth bus wheezed to a stop in front of them. When the door opened like an accordion, they stood for a moment peering in at the driver. "Those rucksacks will have to be stowed down below," he called out gravely. So he was not a mirage. "A bit cold, like," he observed while shoving the packs into the luggage hold in the belly of the bus. "There's two seats for you in the back, and lap rugs overhead. We reach Edinburgh at five-forty." He spoke with the weightiness of a sea captain discussing an ocean passage.

Hazard smelled travel-worn bodies and damp wool as he moved down the aisle of the bus. Murmurs, snores, underwater burbling. In the feeble light the heads of the other passengers looked like charred stumps. By the rear window, where the exhaust fumes seemed dense enough to float in, they found two seats. The lap rugs proved to be tartan blankets, sumptuous foretokens of Scotland.

"It's worth being cold just to cuddle under one of these," Sierra whispered.

"So cuddle up with your favorite stoic," Hazard whispered back, swollen with contentment now. Amazing, that a ticket purchased in Cambridge had made this machine halt for them in the middle of nowhere, in the middle of the night. Sierra's breath smelled faintly of jasmine. Beneath the woolen blankets, his fingers searched out the waistband of her jeans.

She clamped her hand down over his groping fingers. "Not till you warm up those icy paws. Meanwhile, hand over the eyedrops."

Hazard stopped chafing his palms together. "They're down in the whale's belly, inside my pack."

"In your *pack*? You really do want to go blind. We've got to stop this bus."

When she started to rise, he grabbed her by the wrist and squeezed, meaning to hurt. "If you raise a ruckus, I'll get off and walk back to Memphis, I swear it."

"Sure you will. Blind. Across the ocean."

He did not answer, but he kept his grip on her wrist. Then her stillness made him ashamed, and he let her go. "I'm sorry, I can't stand to have people bothering over me."

"Why not?"

"It's just the way I'm made."

"The way you're made is pigheaded," she snapped.

In the seat in front of theirs, a body stirred heavily and a baby whimpered. A woman's voice, ragged with exhaustion, cooed and lullabied. But the baby would not be comforted and the whimpers soon turned to howls.

More quietly, her voice crowded with anger, Sierra said, "You're suffering from a superman complex."

"The baby," Hazard whispered, finger to lips.

"You won't take medicine, won't take money, won't take help. You won't even take love when you need it most. Touch me not!"

The baby's wailing shushed her. Wrapping herself in the blanket from ankle to neck, barricaded against his fumbling apologetic hands, Sierra turned away from him toward the aisle and pretended to sleep. Within a few minutes she really was sleeping.

Hazard stared out the window at the rhomboids of light dragged along the ground by the bus. But soon his eyes throbbed so painfully that he had to squeeze them shut. Fool, Hazard, you stubborn fool. Of course he didn't want to go blind. He didn't want to get along without her, couldn't get along without her. It was just that whenever she tried to prop him up, to lead him this way or that, he laid back his ears and balked, just like one of his grandfather's Mississippi mules.

The baby's crying rose and fell, pitched from octave to octave, playing through all the registers of discontent. It's not anguish, Hazard tried to persuade himself. Babies simply cry; they're made to cry. Yet he could not shut out the mournful wailing. It clawed at some tissue in his brain. If only he could clutch the baby and carry it around tucked under his chin, as he used to carry his youngest sister, singing ballads about moonshiners and lonesome freight trains, he'd soon have it purring.

When Hazard next opened his eyes, they felt like two coals burning in his face. Between the seats he could see that the mother had the baby stomach-down across her lap, and was rubbing its back with her palm. It doesn't want that, he thought; it wants to be squeezed with both arms against a chest, hear a heartbeat, be saved from this growling night-ride among strangers. Unable to stand the wailing any longer, he leaned forward and murmured, "Maybe I could carry her up and down the aisle."

The mother grappled the baby to her, rocking back and forth with a low moaning that sounded like the bus tires on the road.

"I'm used to babies," he said.

The woman's dog-tired face turned around and gave him a look as if he had offered to disembowel the child instead of comfort it.

She turned away again without speaking. Hazard would have paid cash money right then to hold that baby. But he didn't have the money, and he didn't have the nerve. Squeezing a fistful of the tartan blanket in each hand, he pressed the cloth against his ears. Muffled by the wool, the baby's cry and the mother's crooning blended with the steady thrum of the bus. Just before he closed his eyes, he saw through the window the first dusting of snow, like powdered sugar on the black earth. The last thing he felt before sleep was Sierra's head nuzzling against him, her fingers creeping between the buttons of his shirt. Her breathing was as rhythmic as a dulcimer strum.

Next thing he knew, Sierra was nibbling at his throat. "We're in Edinburgh, you Lazybones Jones. Stir a foot." Luggage was grating down from the overhead rack, bodies were lurching past. No road sounds, no mournful baby.

His eyes would not open. Touching, he found the lids encrusted with mucus, the lashes gritty.

"Don't rub," Sierra warned. "Oh yuck, what a mess. First thing we're going to do after we get unloaded here is plunk in some of those drops."

"But I can't get them open."

"Let the witchdoctor have a look." Her fingers gingerly brushed at the mattering along his lids. She smelled of sleep and stillness. "Now try."

This time he managed to force the eyes open. Two knife wounds. He howled, squeezing them shut and clamping his teeth against the pain.

"We've got to get you a doctor," she said in alarm.

"He'll only just fish around with his flashlight, and give me the same prescription the guy in Cambridge did."

"Will you let me put in the medicine, then?"

"I guess."

"All right. Can you see well enough to get off the bus?"

"Sure, sure. They're a little sore, is all. They'll be okay after I use them a while."

"Button up, then. There's six inches of snow outside. And let me fold that gorgeous blanket." He felt the laprug slither across his legs. "Try to imagine anything half so handsome on a bus in America."

"How's the baby? I don't hear it."

"It already got off, poor thing. The mother looked as if she'd just rowed across the Atlantic. They should put her face on birth-control posters." Hazard sat listening to her stupidly, hands dangling slack between his knees, paralyzed by the fire in his eyes. "Up with the hood, now. Tie the string under the little chinny-chin. That's right. Now on with the mittens. What a good boy!" Sierra's laugh was the warmest sound he had heard since the organist clapped his keyboard shut. "Maybe we should hold off on having babies," she said, "until I've finished raising you."

Irked by that, feeling again like a balky mule, Hazard surged to his feet, and nearly knocked himself senseless on the luggage rack. Sierra groped for his hand, but he drew back from her and said, "Go on, go on. Baby will follow."

With eyes slitted open and head tilted back, he could just barely keep track of her brisk legs in front of him. The driver was dishing out luggage, calling the names of passengers with his sea captain's bravado. Beside the front wheel their rucksacks leaned against one another like two drunks, like two mourners — like his grandparents after fifty years of marriage. Sierra already had the eyedrops out. "Sit down on this bench," she ordered him. "Head on my lap. Fine. Okay now, left eye first, good and wide." He forced the lid open with his fingers, and the drops seared down on his eye like boiling grease. "Now the right. That's it. There, now." Squeezing the sides of the bench, he tried to keep his legs from twitching; but for a few seconds his boot heels thumped against the wood. Then the medicine caught hold, the numbness arrived. He realized from the way her fingers were slicking across his cheeks that he had been crying, and he lifted his head from her lap at once.

"Right," he blustered. "Let's see the city." He dried his face with the backs of his rabbitskin gloves.

"You've got no business looking at anything with those eyes," she said. "You need to keep the medicine in them and keep them shut so they can heal."

"Where's the map? Where's the *Blue Guide*?" He tried to stand up, but she pushed down on his shoulders.

"Just sit, I'll get them," she said. "At least keep your eyes closed while I dope out the walking tour." He could hear the scuffle of the rucksacks as she dragged them to the bench, then the abrupt sizzle of a zipper, the crinkle of the map unfolding. "Will it kill you to have somebody look after you once in a while?"

"So read the map."

She was silent for a moment. He knew she was studying him. Then she said, "Okay, here's the bus station, and that must be Princes Street. So Holyrood Castle is down that way, and the palace is up at that end." She nattered on about streets and parks and museums, full of eagerness. Her fingernail made a skittering noise on the map as she traced their itinerary. It was hard to follow her voice amid the din of bus horns, loudspeakers, diesel engines. Finally she announced that the all-time premier one-day walking tour of Edinburgh was doped out. She made him sit tight while she stashed the rucksacks in a locker. When she came back she handed him a cold slick ball — an orange, his nose told him — and said, "Here's the first installment on breakfast."

As he followed her out of the station, eyes cracked open just enough to see the glistening lamplit sidewalks, he peeled the orange with bare hands, stuffing the rind in his pocket. Each time he bit down on a section of the fruit he wondered how far these juices had traveled to reach him before dawn in this frozen city.

Very few cars crunched through the snowglazed streets. Here and there a shop window was lit. Men unloading trucks at the curb hefted cartons and sacks onto their shoulders. A pair of shivering dogs nosed at trashcans.

Sierra talked her way into a bakery that was not yet officially open, and purchased there half a dozen hot rolls. From a horsedrawn milk-cart rumbling over the cobblestones on its morning rounds she bought a slab of butter. "Spare no expense!" she cried gaily. So they ate butter-drenched rolls with mugs of hot chocolate at a café. Hazard could no longer see to record the prices on the card in his wallet. At every halt in the early-morning walk, he shut his eyes. Closed, they let his mind attend to other things. But when they were open even a slit, their fire obliterated all other sensations.

"You look like a basket case," Sierra informed him at the café.

"And feel like one," he admitted.

"Why don't you just leave them closed and I'll lead you around?"

"I'll see a fat lot of Edinburgh that way."

"I can tell you about things."

"Be my seeing-eye dog?"

"Woof, woof!"

He laughed, eyes closed, playing the blind man. Clink of spoons against saucers. Burr on all the Scottish voices. The table still felt damp from its morning once-over with the washrag.

But in the street again, forcing his eyes open, he pulled his arm free of her guiding hand. "I'm all right. Where to first?"

Instead of answering, she went huffing away down the sidewalk, salt and ice scrunching beneath her boots.

Hazard could not keep up with her. In his watery daze he shouldered into a man who was rolling a barrel with his foot. Then as Sierra nipped across a street he stumbled on the curb and fell sprawling. Brutal smack of pavement on wrists, elbows, chin. Tires grinding to a halt near his head. Sierra's hands under his arm, dragging him upright.

"You'll get yourself killed! You and your he-man independence." She thumped the snow from his coat and pants, harder than she needed to, hard enough to make him stagger to keep his balance. "Hazard," she scolded, gripping him fiercely just above his left elbow, "if you won't keep your eyes shut and let me guide you, I'm going to go sit in the bus station and not budge. If you want to stumble under a truck, go right ahead."

In his temporary darkness, Hazard rehearsed the advice of his father and grandfather. Then he fought down his mulish instinct, saying, "You lead."

So he shambled along beside her through the frozen city — stiffly, reluctantly, feeling the turns he was supposed to make by the pressure of her fingers on his arm, listening to her tell about what there was to see. The awkwardness reminded him of learning to waltz, when his mother had swooped him around the living room to the strains of his father's fiddling. But he had eventually learned to dance like a dervish. And now he found himself relaxing in Sierra's grip.

Mercifully shut, his eyes quit pestering him, and the noises and smells and tastes of the city wafted through him. The cold air smacked of coal smoke. Tires gritted rhythmically on the cobbled streets. Sierra's voice sang in his ears, painting visions for him: Princes Street, the gardens with shrubs like white-capped penguins; clouds of breath around the muzzles of horses pulling the occasional wagon; children passing on their way to school in little chattering armadas, like ducks; sooty buildings with stairstepped gables.

"Here's the monument to Sir Walter Scott," she announced. "And it's everything our friend the organist said it would be. Two hundred feet tall, according to the book. It looks to me like a giant lob-lolly pine turned upside down, with the limbs at the bottom. Or maybe a Saturn rocket. And underneath here, let's see, is a statue of Sir Walter himself. They've even got his dog in there with him. Around the sides there's a bunch of little statues—must be characters from his works, a very passionate crew by the looks of them. The whole gigantic tower's more fretted and frilly than a doily."

A fantastic Edinburgh grew inside him, nurtured by her words. After a few hours of listening he lost all awareness of her voice, and perceived directly whatever she described. He no longer felt her fingers on his arm, but seemed to be fused with her, a four-legged animal. Walking came to feel like dancing, a yielding to music.

In the palace she read to him from the guidebook: a threnody of murders, invasions, and butcheries, relieved only by her comic asides. In the National Gallery she appraised the Titians, the Watteaus, the Gainsboroughs ("This woman here with a peachbasket hat and feather trimmings looks like a bored kitchen-appliances demonstrator"), the acres of portraits. In the Royal Scottish Museum she guided his hand so that he could touch the marble flesh of the statues.

Only when she sat him down on a park bench and gently pried his eyes open for the next dose of eyedrops did he retreat into his own body. The scalding pain was briefer this time. He was in no hurry to lift his head from her lap.

"They're not looking so bloodshot," she observed. "Keep this up the rest of today, and I might let you open them tomorrow. I might even agree to marry you."

That sat him bolt upright. "What brought that up?"

"Has it ever been put away?"

"But why right this minute?"

Her fingers spidered across his forehead. "Just you, the way you're letting me lead you around. Your tender side isn't all that bad, when you let it come out of hiding."

"I'll show you my tender side!" he bellowed with mock ferocity, groping toward her voice with strangler's hands.

"Eyes shut!" she cried. He could hear her leaping from the bench and skipping away a few paces over the snowpacked walk. "Can't catch me, I'm the gingerbread woman!"

Arms outspread like a lateshow monster, he lurched blindly after her. By calling to him she led him bump against a tree, a lamp-post, a fire hydrant, her laugh giddying high above his. Then after she had been silent for half a minute, he nudged forward against softness and felt her arms closing around him, and her lips on his face.

Following the organist's advice, they climbed up to the castle an hour before sunset, her hand on his arm, her voice supplying his vision. "What we're standing on here, says the book, is the site of an Iron Age fort. It was the home of the unlucky Mary Queen of Scots, and the birthing place of James the First and other bigwigs. The blood's soaked nine feet into the basalt rock, by actual measure."

She described the bejeweled crowns, the gold-hilted swords, the armor—some of which, she told him, looked as if it had been hammered out of tin cookie-sheets. Then she led him into a chamber of the castle where her voice reverberated off the stone walls. "Here's the Scottish War Memorial," she whispered. The other conversations he could hear were also muted. "There're flags overhead," she murmured, "and uniforms pinned up on the walls. And here's a great big book inside a glass case, filled with names of the dead."

Just then the hush was shattered by a brusque clicking of heels over the floor. The sound clattered straight toward Hazard, then stopped. A harsh military voice declared, "Sir, this is a holy place, and you will please uncover your head."

"Of course, I didn't realize," Hazard stammered, fumbling the hood back, tugging loose the knitted cap.

"Officious bully," Sierra hissed. Squeezing Hazard's arm protectively, she led him away.

After a few seconds the clicking heels approached again, but this time hesitantly. The voice was softened into a lovely Scottish singsong: "I'm so very sorry, sir. I didna realize your condition."

"It's nothing," Hazard reassured him.

"But it was a terrible rudeness. Here, let me open this case for you. Here now, run your hands over the page. Can you feel the ink?"

Hazard shied back from the man's touch, not wanting his sympathy, not wanting him to feel bad. "I'm not blind. It's just a soreness keeps them shut, some kind of infection."

The man's voice, minty, came from a few inches away now. "Infection, is it? Here, let's have a look." Before Hazard could flinch away there were fingers prodding one lid open. "Aye, that's your redeye, that is. I know it from the war. North Africa. Douse it with salt water, is what you do. Be gone in a week."

Suddenly the hand jerked away and Sierra was bawling, "Leave him alone! Can't you see he's in pain?"

"It doesn't matter," Hazard tried to explain. But Sierra was dragging him away.

Outside the chapel she huffed, "Bully! Poking at a blind man."

"I'm *not* blind."

"Did he know that? He's got no business prying at you as if you were chucksteak. He ought to have his thumbs broken. You put a uniform on a man and it's instant Napoleon. I should have clobbered him."

"It's over," he soothed. "Forget it."

She took a great calming breath, let it out, muttered into silence. They walked across the castle grounds until their footsteps no longer struck echoes from the walls, until their bodies danced in that single-animal harmony. The air tasted like a stainless steel spoon, it was so cold. Even through the crust of snow, Hazard could sense the uneven tilt of the paving stones. The jitter of traffic sounded impossibly far away. He didn't care where they were headed, didn't think of supper or hotel or Memphis or any other destination, but only let himself blend into the flow of their movement together.

"There's actually a little cemetery here for soldiers' dogs," Sierra told him. Then she gasped. "Good Lord."

"What's the matter?"

"The sunset. It's magnificent."

Hazard waited in darkness for her to describe what she saw. But the only sound she made was a hectic breathing, the way she sometimes panted when making love. "How does it look?" he finally asked.

"Oh, words are useless."

"Try. Tell me."

"Well, the clouds are a flat gray overhead like an iron pot lid, and just above the horizon there's a gap between the clouds and the hills—like a crack in the edge of the world. You can see it whichever way you turn," her boots scuffing around in the snow, "a full circle of light. And in the southwest the bottom of the sun is melting down through the clouds, a fierce crescent of red. You can actually see it dropping, melting through, and the light burnishes all the hills and roofs and treetops. You know, the way faces catch the firelight. And the snow looks like coals, like molten lava slung out over the countryside. Here it comes! The whole sun is burning through the gap now, a great fierce eye. Oh, Hazard, come, turn your face this way," and she took his chin in her hand, aimed his face until he sensed the scarlet glow through his lids. "Just for a second now, open them, open them. It's worth the pain."

And through a haze he glimpsed the fiery landscape, the blazing eye. The earth and sun and sky were all one liquid flame. Sierra's face was tilted up close to his, watching him watch the sun. Her hood was thrown back, and the light streaming through her hair made her seem molten. And he also felt molten, yielded up, set free.

Walking down from the castle terrace with eyes shut again and Sierra's hand on his arm, he caught the distant wail of a bagpipe. Listening, picking out the notes above the sounds of footsteps and traffic, he recognized the tune, a reel his father had taught him to play on the fiddle. The smell of walnut planks and cherry came back to him, and the memory of the wood-handled tools made his fingers curl inside their gloves. He wanted to build fiddles and dulcimers, to finish the pear-wood banjos, and he would let Sierra earn the money so long as she was willing, would let her fold him into her love so long as she would have him.

"Let's go ahead with it," he said, "if you think it's right for you."
Without hesitating, she said, "Marrying?"
"Yes," he said.
"Yes," she answered.

Fetching the Dead

Three thousand miles of water behind it and all the oceans before it, half a continent spreading on either side of it, the Mississippi River — father of all rivers — swept south. Muddy waters roiled against its banks, dissolving clay, gnawing at the unplowed fields. Yet every day another few inches of red clay gaped above the river, for the northern snows had long since melted and the heaviest spring rains had passed. The earth dried.

The clod Morgan held in his hand crumbled as he squeezed. He searched the dusk clouds for signs of tomorrow's weather. The earth was ready; the sun would not wait. He had to plant when the season demanded its seed, even though two sons waited for him in Memphis — one to bring home to work, one to bury.

"I'll have both of them back by morning," he told his wife as he buttoned the suit which had always marked the breaks in their lives — the baptisms, the weddings, and the burials. "Have Joel and Coyt get the mules harnessed and the cows milked so we can plow when we get home — if it don't rain."

Her arms were floured to the elbow with supper. Whatever grief she felt, no sign showed in her face, nor in her body, which fourteen pregnancies and eleven births had swollen. She hobbled back into the kitchen on arthritic ankles as she always hobbled; finished the biscuits, without measure, without recipe, as she made them always. Deaths came as fevers came, as the droughts came, as the rains came.

On the stoop Morgan repeated everything to Joel and Coyt, the

two sons who had stayed on the land. He spoke slowly, gesturing
at each phrase, paring his words and shaping them with his callused
hands, as if dividing what little he knew of the death into pieces small
enough to understand. But when he finished, he knew no more than
when he had begun, nor could he read any explanation in the sun-
dazed stares of his living sons. "Be ready to plow when I get back.
We'll be one short, but we still got to plant. The dead don't alter that."

Joel and Coyt said yessir to their father, and continued to strip
off their sweat-soaked field clothes. "And see that your mother don't
sit up fretting."

As he walked to the shed where the pickup truck was parked,
Morgan wondered which of the sons would quit him next. First Jesse
had gone, and then Ransome. Both had deserted the land that
Morgan had given them, had bucked against the current of the Mississippi River and hungered north to the cities.

The truck radio promised no rain for the next day. Given dry
weather, he could plow. His road to Memphis edged the river, bent
where the river bent, obeyed its contours. Over his shoulder the Mississippi sun, brutally hot even at dusk, melted through layer after
layer of clouds in its slow falling. Across the sun a scatter of ducks
drifted, beating slowly, bound for a destination known only to themselves, and after them a lone duck straggled ever farther behind. The
steady grind of the motor and the late-day heat made Morgan
drowsy. Whenever he tried to think of the son now dead, to discover what this dying meant to him, what adjustment he must make,
his eyes glided on to the river, where debris from floods in the North
caught and carried his mind away. The water bore roofs and doors,
fragments of cities known to him only by name. One of those distant
places had claimed his son. His son, his son, something final had
happened to his son, something called death, but not as cows died,
not as the crops or the year died, some other ending than these: the
cessation of familiar sound, the loss of a hand, the failure of a kidney
or lung. One fewer son to work the land while Morgan lived, one
fewer son to bear his name when he died.

Nearer Memphis the river straightened. Watching its flotsam writhe
in the current, Morgan's thoughts returned to his land. There was
the broken flange on a plow. There was a fresh load of manure to

spread near the creek. There was the gray mule going lame. And there was the one son he hoped would come back from Memphis to help with the planting. The other son, the one who had ceased, that son Morgan closed out of his mind as something unrecoverable, something beyond him.

Ransome,

Now I'm living. Memphis is great. I got me a job making tires, eight hours a day, and it sure beats twelve hours staring at the bony haunches of a mule. And you don't have to feed the machine. I got my own room on the river, and I can see the boats lit up chugging along at night. And Ranse, the women! They swarm like flies up here. Listen, don't bury yourself on that farm. Pa will plow you into that dirt just like he tried to plow me, just like he's plowing the others. Come to Memphis.

Jesse

Clank, clank, clank — the conveyor never paused as the man who had come to relieve Jesse on the night shift took over the controls.

"How's it running?"

"All right," Jesse answered.

"Anything up?"

"Jonas lost an arm."

"Jonas?"

"Second 'A' operator on line 7," Jesse explained.

"That guy who raised camellias?"

"Yeah, him," Jesse answered while recording the production figures on a chart. "See you tomorrow."

"Yeah."

Even though the machines had relinquished him for another day, as he walked to the clock-out alley Jesse unconsciously obeyed their rhythm, stepping in time with every beat of metal on metal. Waiting in the ranks of those leaving at shift change, nodding at the confusion of faces, he slapped the time card against his thigh in rhythm with the factory's pulse. The rhythm carried him to the Mississippi, then shoved him the two dozen blocks upriver to his boarding house.

For all their activity, the barges and freighters could not deflect his memory from that accident: Jesse had seen the rollers seize the man's fingers, watched the man's mouth grope in pain for sounds while the machine tore skin and muscle and bone from the shoulder socket. But over the roar of machinery Jesse had not been able to hear the screams. He did not know whether the man who raised camellias was still alive. If he was, he would be in pain, and Jesse could imagine pain. But he could not imagine what the man had felt seeing a piece of himself ripped away, swallowed by that oblivious piece of machinery, which had duly processed the arm, and had thereby ruined, as the foreman pointed out, eighteen thousand pounds of rubber.

Night after night Jesse dreamed that scene. He had become Jonas, and Jonas's machine had become his machine. In every dream the equipment seized him, but in the instant between seizing and dismembering, he woke. Each time he was dragged to the edge of that final sundering experience, then wakened. At work he became cautious. Once, he was told, a whole man had been mashed through those rollers, had been processed and packaged, bit by bit, in half a trainload of rubber. Hour after hour Jesse watched the loaded conveyor belt disappear between the rollers, then return empty. The longer he watched it, the more he feared it, and the more he feared it, the more he hated it. So one day a few weeks after the accident, he dropped a steel bolt on the conveyor and watched with pleasure as the rollers choked on it, screeched, and finally ripped loose from their bearings.

Before shift change the damage was repaired.

Dreading his equipment at work, fearing those unfinished dreams which possessed him in that room overlooking the river, Jesse thought of returning to his father's farm in Mississippi. Lonely as he had become, however, he could not leave Memphis, unless to go to some larger city. He would go anywhere rather than back to that red dirt farm, do anything, even fight machinery for the rest of his life, rather than slip back into that endless cycle of seasons and crops. His father used to talk of each new crop as possibly his last—either taxes or time would catch up with him. Continual worry about planting and weather and harvest had worn him to the hard kernel of a man, more tool than human, slave to the rhythms of season and soil which he claimed to exploit. Beyond every harvest there was another harvest, endlessly. Jesse could not return to that life. But he had no clear notion of the life which he sought—he only knew that it must be in the cities. There was a current flowing, he sensed that, flowing toward the great northern cities, where there was industry, where there were people, where there was money and change. Let old man Morgan and those muleheaded sons rot in that backwater, let even Ransome stay there if he was a mind to, let the whole Mississippi delta wash into the Gulf of Mexico, Jesse would not go back. His country was on the move, and though he did not know where or why, he would move with it.

At a bend in the road, the coffin slid across the truck bed. Morgan glanced in the mirror. He had forgotten why he was driving to Memphis; at least he had ceased to think of the boy who would fill that box on the return journey. The coffin was only pine, but it was good pine, the last of the thick-barked loblolly he had cut from the riverbottom and carted to Amory sawmill twenty-eight years before, when building his marriage house. Those tight-grained planks, cured in the barnloft, would leak no water. His son would be safe in them. The body of his son. The body—whatever that was—of his son—whoever and wherever he was.

Fear shoved Morgan's foot down on the accelerator. Beyond the feeble spray of his headlights was blackness, no sign of houses, no other traffic, nothing to reassure him during one terrified minute that he was actually moving, that he would ever emerge on the other side of night into Memphis to recover a dead son, or even that he himself was still alive. The pickup strained against his mounting fear. And then he slowed, for something in the darkness had gleamed in answer to the headlights. It was the river, shimmering and pitching southwards. There at least was something certain, something to reckon by—the current of the Mississippi. Afterwards even when he could not see the river, when all other landmarks had dissolved back into the darkness, when the truck-lights reflected on nothing, still Morgan sensed that nearby massive current laboring south. That one motion, in this night made strange by his son's death, seemed to him absolute, and therefore comforting.

Ransome,

   Look, Pa's got you under his thumb and Ma's got you tied to her apron strings. When are you going to grow up and see they don't give a damn about you, all they give a damn about are those 327 acres? It takes you one hell of a time to make up that scrawny mind of yours. I've waited two months for you to decide whether you're coming up north with me, or what. Now listen, I've got two tickets on a bus for Chicago that leaves next Friday afternoon, that's the 17th. If you're here, we can go together. If you don't come, there's others who'd jump at the chance.

Jesse

   Two men slick with sweat under the glaring electric lights mechanically loaded bags of rice into the boxcar. They held each bag by its two ears, lifted, swung, all as regular and shiny as robots in the corrosive light. Ransome watched for a few minutes just outside the circle of lights (one hand shoved into his pocket, the other dangling a rumpled paper sack), then passed on down the tracks. Although the sides of the rails had rusted, continual switching of trains had polished their surfaces silver. Between the cross-ties grease had soaked the humped gravel roadbed, which like an endless snake lifted the tracks off the flat, naked Mississippi river-lands.

   Several times as he walked down the tracks Ransome patted the soiled, dog-eared letter which stuck out of his shirt pocket, as if to make certain he still had it. *Like Jesse wrote just find me an empty boxcar and crawl back in the corner where the brakeman don't see me,* he thought, *and in four hours I'm there.*

   "This the train to Memphis?" he asked a man in a dingy railroad uniform.

   "Yeah, but ain't no passengers on this run. Next passenger leaves out at seven." The man stumped away, copying into a notebook numbers from the wood blocks on the doors of boxcars, blocks which were riddled with staples from hundreds of destinations those cars had borne.

   Like Jesse says if I don't clear out now I'll be walking over that land till I wear ruts in it and bury myself like Pa. He can make do without me and there's Joel and Coyt and the girls to look after Ma. I can hear Pa tomorrow morning saying he's a damn fine worker

and a good son and I just don't believe he'd ever run off and leave
them who reared him. And Ma saying my baby's gone my Ransome.
But Jesse says Chicago is some roaring place and the times he says
O Ransome the times we'll have. Come Ransome because this whole
land is on the move and if we stand still it will move on without us.

Thick steel springs coiled over the heavy flanged wheels of the boxcars. Ransome counted the massive steel couplings, the rubber-coated
wires, the iron-lace platforms that jutted from the ends of cars, as
he walked farther down the track away from the light and stir of
the station. On the sides of cars names stood in letters half as high
as a man: UNION PACIFIC, SANTA FE, SOUTHERN STATES, NEW YORK
CENTRAL, ERIE & PENNSYLVANIA. Ransome read the names and wondered; they were still just words to him, places by hearsay. For him
that wonder had always attached to the railroad, with its ponderous
grace, its plumes of steam and bruising speed, with its cars that could
have come from anywhere and could be going anywhere. Tonight
he was bound for Memphis, and yet he might wake tomorrow in a
city whose name he had never heard.

During his last eight hours at the rubber factory Jesse watched
the conveyors and rollers with a special wariness. Listening to the
rhythms of the machinery, mesmerized by the unvarying motions
of his own piece of equipment, dazed by fumes and heat from the
drying furnaces, Jesse frequently imagined that the entire factory
was insanely alive, yet that it was only a single organ incorporated
in some monstrous host whose vast life the interchangeable workers
somehow remotely sustained. Sometimes he even imagined (as he
still dreamed at night) that the factory would not relinquish him,
but would seize him in a careless moment and transform him, as
it had transformed Jonas's arm, into rubber. After obeying the same
machinery for months, it was hard to believe that in a few hours
he would be free, that he could meet his brother on the train from
Mississippi, catch the bus north and start a new life in Chicago. He
waited cautiously for the final horn.

When shift change came, he left his goggles and helmet in the
locker and walked with relief into the spring-warm streets. Eight

months earlier, when he had watched from his belly atop a Union Pacific freighter chuffing into the city, Memphis had been a wonder. The traffic, the store windows and advertisements and sharp angles of concrete, all the intricate and mysterious trappings of the city in motion, the swarms of people who choked sidewalks every day of the week including Sunday, the dazzling hodgepodge of people drifting through Memphis from the Mississippi River, from the North or even from farther away, the frantic construction of office buildings and factories, the feverish signs of wealth and growth had bewildered and amazed him. Compared to Memphis his hometown in Standler, Mississippi, was only a crossroads. Enough houses, stores, grain elevators, cotton gins and gas stations had accumulated during the century of Standler's existence to line both sides of a half-mile stretch of macadam road. Beyond that was the prairie. So Memphis had seemed to Jesse a vast and frenzied place; yet in eight months of roaming her streets he thought he had seen all there was to see, and he was ready to move on. St. Louis was too near and New York was too far, so there was Chicago, Chicago with its lake you couldn't see across, its stockyards, its railroads, its riches, its expanse.

Now finally, after eight months of working in this miraculous city, walking streets glutted with strange faces, waiting, forever waiting, with no one definite to see and no place definite to go, Jesse had a brother to meet. Ransome was coming. Jesse felt he was regaining part of himself, for the brothers were like extensions of the same person, sharing an awed rebellion against their ironminded and proud father, the youngest sons of the family, ninth and tenth children to that ponderous woman who for fifteen years had borne Abe Morgan one baby after another, as regular as cotton harvesting, as sturdy as the plowing mules.

For nineteen years the two brothers had been inseparable: two shapes moving off over the fields toward fishing or courting or fertilizing, two faces at the table, two redheads plastered sleek with grease for Saturday nights in town. Both played the harmonica, knew all the same songs, told the same jokes, manufactured the same stories, fought and worked and played together. They looked so much alike that they could swap new girlfriends without being detected. From a distance even their parents confused them — unless the boys were walking, for Jesse always strutted a bit more, always looked the cockier of the two.

The brothers had been inseparable until eight months earlier, when Jesse had said let's go to Memphis, get out of these damned sunburnt fields and make our way in the City. And Ransome had said no, Morgan needed him, his mother needed him. And so Jesse had gone to Memphis alone. But now Ransome was coming. Jesse had persuaded him to break with his parents, to leave the land, and follow.

Ransome leapt onto the bed of the boxcar and closed the door behind him. As he sat in the close darkness, waiting for the train to move, distinguishing the smells of cattle and rice, wheat and oil and men which the car had carried, he thought he heard some sound, some invisible stealthy movement in the blackness. He listened intently, shutting off all noises from outside the boxcar, concentrating with an intensity which he would not admit as fear on the sound near him in the darkness.

Yes — breathing.

Ransome turned abruptly in the direction from which he thought the breathing came, and he noticed for the first time the red point of a cigarette like an unblinking eye staring at him.

"Which way we headed?" a voice asked. The glow of the cigarette bobbed. The walls of the boxcar confused the sound.

Is it a nigger? Ransome thought.

"Memphis." He had to squint to make out an indistinct, withered, ashen face behind the burning cigarette. "Why you riding if you don't know where it's heading?"

"Just riding."

"Don't matter where?"

"Don't much matter which way, so long as we just get moving. Memphis is as good a place as anywheres else."

It is a nigger, Ransome thought, *an old nigger, old as the hills.* Fingers lifted beneath the cigarette, clinched it, drew it away, and then returned it to the lips. The gaunt face was a weathered gray that shaded into the darkness. *What's he doing in this boxcar?*

There was a heavy thud on the roof, and Ransome jumped nervously. Footsteps stamped across the roof the length of the boxcar, then disappeared. The other man laughed gently. "The brakeman. He don't bite."

"What you laughing at?" Ransome snapped.

"The way you jumping. Relax. Pull up a sack and set on your butt into Memphis. The brakeman can't do nothing but throw us off if he *do* find us, and if he *don't,* you might just as well be comfortable."

Ransome folded an empty feed sack and sat on it. Beyond the door there was a quickening release of air, the heavy chuffing of the engine far up beyond the station, and then the rising beat of steel wheels on the tracks as the train accelerated northwards, toward Memphis. Lulled by the throb of the rails, Ransome temporarily forgot about the other man; in fact, when the cigarette vanished and the sound of breathing succumbed to the racket of the train, he almost doubted whether the other man were really still there, invisible and silent in the darkness. So he was startled when the old Negro spoke.

"What you figuring on doing up yonder?"

"Got a brother there. We're going to Chicago."

"Yeah, but what you gonna *do* when you get to Chicago?"

"I don't know," Ransome said, slightly irritated.

"Oh." The old man separated every two statements by a gully of silence. In a moment, he spoke again.

"Going all the way to Chicago and you don't know *why?*"

Defensively now, Ransome tried to account for himself: "Well, likely we'll get us a job, meet some women, have us a time. I don't know. We ain't there yet."

"A body don't have to go half way across the country to do *that.* Sounds like you and your brother just be itching to move. I know all about moving."

"You got a mighty long nose, sticking it in other people's business."

"Easy, easy." The old man's voice was resonant in the boxcar. After a few minutes of silence, quietly, he resumed. "You ain't too old—are you?"

Underneath them the brutal pulse of the wheels pounding the tracks.

"Old enough," Ransome answered.

"You're green."

"I'm not as near dead as you are," Ransome nearly shouted.

"How old?"

"Look, what is this—you writing a book?"

"You got a long ride ahead of you," the old man said, and laughed to himself.

"What's so damned funny?" Ransome said sharply, and then—as if surprised by the loudness of his own voice in the boxcar—more quietly: "I reckon I'm old enough to go when I want and come when I want."

"I reckon you are, I reckon you are. I wasn't laughing at you. I was laughing at me." Just when Ransome thought the old man had finished and was content to ride in silence, the voice resumed.

"I started when I was younger than you, when I was fourteen, and I been riding ever since." Again the long space of silence, broken by a deep breath and the voice resuming. "My old man was a share-cropper and weren't nothing else *I* could be. But I couldn't stand seeing him broke down by it and so I lit out." He seemed to forget what he had been saying, or to remember more than he could say. "Yessir, that's what *I'm* running from. That life. That goddamn man-killing life." His voice gradually softened, as if tired, as if years of use had worn it thin like the man talking. "What you be running from?"

"Nothing!" Ransome shouted. Then, startled again by his own shout, he fell abruptly silent.

"Oh," the old Negro said.

For a long while the two sat silent. The old man lit another cigarette. In the matchlight the gaunt face seemed drawn, harried, ancient, and yet somehow beyond hunger and age. To Ransome the face and the voice suggested vast time and distance. Despite his irritation, he was fascinated and felt the old man's travels must have carried him places he himself had never dreamed of. The old man seemed to move in a dimension which Ransome feared he would never grow into. Almost against his will, he finally asked: "Where all have you been?"

"Everywhere and nowhere." He rattled off the names of states and cities like the words of a song. "But that ain't a fraction. There's a damn sight more country than a man thinks the first time he crawls into a boxcar. You ain't never going to see it *all.*"

Ransome stared at the cigarette tip, which glowed and dimmed in rhythm with the other man's breath, watched the minute fire finally waver and die, and thought, *It ain't true. I'm running from nobody. When the current moves a man has to move with it like Jesse says.* Another match flared. *It ain't true ain't true ain't true.* The man looked at Ransome over the cupped match:

"You scared, boy?"

"No I'm not scared, and I ain't *boy* neither!"

The man took a long drag on the cigarette. "Why, you sure do *look* at me scared."

Ransome struggled to keep his voice steady. "They ain't nothing scary about you." *Spooky old nigger. I'll throw his old ass off this train. He's got no business on it anyways.*

"You just looking worried, that's all, and you ain't got no call looking scared at me." Ransome could hear his hands rustling about in the dark, searching for something.

"What you after?" Ransome demanded. *He got a knife?*

"Something."

"*What?*" Ransome crouched, ready to leap aside.

"Something to give you." The hands stopped searching and lifted quickly between him and Ransome.

"Watch it!" Ransome sprung to his feet.

"Easy, easy now. What's bit you? Here—." Ransome could vaguely see the old man's hand reaching out towards him in the dark—"You want a slice of bread?"

"Bread?"

"Yeah, bread."

Ransome reached out uncertainly to touch the coarse bread in the man's outstretched palm. "No thanks. I ain't hungry." He squatted back down and his fists relaxed, but he still stared uneasily at the old man in the dark.

"Well I'll just leave it here for later. You might get hungry."

"I won't."

"That's up to you."

Ransome could not stop watching the blurred shadow of the other man's face. In the darkness for a moment it seemed smooth and kindly, almost fatherly. But only for a moment. The tension between them persisted. Slowly, slowly, like static accumulating from friction on the rails, the tension increased. It was something bewildering but fierce in him, something older than he was, some hatred or fear grafted on to his fathers, that swelled up in him against the other man. He could not understand it, the tension building across their silence, but he could feel it, and he thought he could see it in the other man's face, in the other man's movements, the two hands invisible in the dark.

With a sudden jolt the brakes caught and the train slowed to a stop. They had not traveled far enough to be in Memphis yet.

"Switching," the old man explained.

They heard the door of the car in front of them roll heavily open, and then rumble shut. Boots crunched over the gravel toward them. Ransome scrambled to his feet.

"Set still," the old man whispered. "Likely he won't look for more than one. They're stupid, these jokers." He rose quickly and walked to the door. "You get on up to Memphis, son, or on to Chicago, but then you set still. Don't keep moving. There's no end of railroads. Now take it easy."

The door rumbled open. A squat man looking official in a shabby uniform lifted a lantern into the Negro's face.

"So long, boss. Thanks for the lift," the old man said as he leapt past the signalman and scrambled down the gravel roadbed.

"Why the black son—" the signalman swore. But the old man had already disappeared laughing into the dark. Still swearing, the signalman lifted his lantern over the bed of the boxcar, glanced quickly around and, apparently satisfied, slammed the door heavily.

Ransome relaxed against the wall and listened to the engine far up the line urging the train back into motion. The heavy steel pulse of the tracks gradually rose. Now when it was too late he wanted the old Negro back, to ask him about the places he'd seen, to find out what was inside him. *What's he mean calling me scared? And telling me to sit still when he's going to go on and on till he drops? He's a puzzle.* He fumbled around for the bread, sniffed it briefly, and then slowly ate it. *And him jumping off and leaving me to ride. Leaving me on to get to Memphis and eat his food. He was all right*

*not just for a nigger but all right for a man. I'll tell Jesse I run into
a good old man.*

If he'd stayed home he'd be alive now, Morgan thought. From
time to time for about an hour he had been glancing over his right
shoulder as he drove, waiting for the sun. *If they'd had to work as
hard for their land as I did they'd never've left it. They don't remember the worst years. It was my cotton rotted in thirty-one, but they
always ate. It's my barn was mortgaged, and my tractor, but they
never went naked. Four years later and there's jobs in the cities. They
think it's always been like this.* Already the early morning traffic
thickened towards Memphis, and it frightened him, for it moved too
swiftly. The cars and trucks hustling each other left him no time for
decision, for his thought like his speech was deliberate, every adjustment of mind or emotion was labored, his whole life was attuned
to gradual changes. *I wouldn't want them farming all their lives,
wouldn't wish that on a dog, but it's good enough to give them a
start. It's been good enough to feed them. But they were just too
big to work for their daddy and too smart to learn from him.*
As the sun cleared the Tennessee hills, the river, which had gleamed
like spun silver in the headlights the night before, appeared more
and more clearly as the muddy, gorged torrent it had been all along.
Nearing Memphis, the road veered from the river, yet Morgan remained aware of its dark, furious current running parallel and
counter to his own route. *But why'd they sneak away like whipped
dogs? Why didn't they tell me they had to go?* Dodging uneasily
through the glutted Memphis streets, he added up all the accumulated leavings of his life, in land and money, in buildings, in children and memories, and with these achievements he defended himself
against those two sons who had repudiated his work, his way of life,
his purposes. Yet one gap in the defense he could not fill, for one
child had claimed another promise from America, had turned forever
against his father, for that child was dead, and could not be reclaimed.

Two hours later Ransome woke up. The train had stopped.
Memphis, he thought, *this has got to be Memphis. Just find Jesse
and I'm all right. Just find Jesse.*

He opened the door, jumped out, and walked toward the engine and the tight cluster of lights that swarmed the station house.

"We at Memphis?" he asked a baggage porter.

"Nosir, this here's Tunica, Mississippi."

"Does that train go on to Memphis?" Ransome jerked his head towards the single line of boxcars he had just left.

"Not till morning—about eight," the porter answered.

"Is there any other I can catch?"

"There's a passenger comes through in half an hour—but it don't stop." He started to move away, then hesitated, smiling broadly, and said: "But it slows down . . ." Ransome watched him waddle away to the loading platform, then turned and walked in the opposite direction, north of the station along the tracks. He reached a thick stand of pines where he waited for the passenger train to come through, for he knew it would have to slow there for a curve, and he could jump a ride into Memphis.

I'm coming fast as I can Jesse. Ma and Pa will raise all kind of sand but I'm coming Jesse cause we got to get out got to make it on our own. Like you say the land will break us like it broke Pa and like it's breaking Joel and Coyt. The two of us we can make it in Chicago. He leaned against the rough trunk of a pine and waited, waited, as if he had been waiting all his life for this one train to slow down in front of him and carry him to manhood. *And that old man in the boxcar you got to hear about him Jesse and all his bull about sitting still.*

Watching the river traffic surging down from the north and churning back from the south, wondering what the barges and steamers bore, waiting for eleven o'clock so that he could go to the station to meet his brother, Jesse tried to imagine their life together in Chicago. Memphis had failed. He could not return to a factory, now that he had escaped, for the monstrous indifference of the machinery and the brutality of the work itself had frightened him. Even in Memphis he felt tiny. Every day he worked, every dollar he spent disappeared without trace into the chaotic ferment of the city. His life seemed to leave no mark anywhere. And Chicago might be only a larger version of Memphis. Yet he felt he had to go, for the only alternative seemed to be the land, and he felt that America was becoming a nation of cities, that whatever future there was would be in the cities. A man couldn't earn a living at hunting or fishing, and the army was no good because who wanted to be a stiff-backed old monkey like Uncle Lycurgus with his box of medals and his head cluttered with the world war like an attic full of busted furniture. There was nothing but the cities.

On a barge decorated with colored lights a jazz band played defiantly into the limitless vacuum of the night, and dozens of couples frantically danced.

So he would go to Chicago, without knowing why, without knowing what he would do when he arrived, because he sensed the current of men flowing there, and because at twenty the one thing he owned was the future.

Walking, walking, soon windows square with yellow lights riddled the tall black shell of the train station directly ahead of him.

Damn the factory and damn the farm we can leave now Ranse. Won't be any more wrestling with the damned earth and if the whole cotton crop is burnt to hell it won't make a wood nickel difference. Won't be any more punching cards and writing numbers and counting your fingers after work to make sure they're all still hanging on. Brother we may be running but when a man stops running he's dead brother. And one thing I'm never going to be is dead.

Jesse walked through a tunnel under the tracks, and came out onto the platform where he waited, hands in pockets, smoking.

Your train Ranse. Brother in that train with all the steel wheels grinding and the brakes hissing and the smoke. O brother your train Ranse your train.

Ransome stood still, waiting, a long shadow among long shadows in the tall march of slash pines that bordered the Santa Fe tracks. Away south—back toward his home where they would be missing him, where his mother certainly would be sitting up worrying over her youngest son—away south he heard the fierce, whining rush of a night train. He heard the whistle scream as the train pounded its way into Tunica, the whistle shrieking without an echo, a sound that spread and spread forever into the black Mississippi River flatlands.

Ransome thought he felt the earth trembling, would not admit that he himself was trembling, could not stop thinking *Jesse said don't you ever shag one Ransome don't you ever. You don't know how you fool kid. Just find you an empty boxcar and crawl in but don't ever try shagging a train. And I saying yes Jesse yes I won't ever but I got to get to you got to get to Memphis.*

Now the earth was trembling and Ransome trembled with it.

Black, violent, dragging its passenger cars filled with lights and faces, the train slowed ponderously for the curve in the rails immediately in front of the pine wood. Ransome trotted out toward the tracks. He reached the gravel roadbed. The long narrow cone of the headlight ripped across the pine trunks, then tilted up for a moment into the night sky, reflecting nothing, a straight finger probing blindly into the black sky, as the locomotive pounded through the curve.

Ransome you're a man you got to move you got to jump at that train.

He crept up to within a few feet of the rushing cars. The train was gaining speed again. The steel pulse rose. *It's going to leave you.* He could see the caboose approaching, a dozen cars back. *Jump coward jump.* The gravel shuddered under the massive cars. The wheels pounded and squealed over the rails. He edged closer. *Jump jump jump.* He crouched, hesitated one terrified moment, aimed at a ladder on the trailing edge of a baggage car, and sprang—

Brother here I come O God I come

The train registered nothing. There was no hitch in its motion. Not even a tremor.

"I seen him go under. Just like a doll or a piece of rag. It was two cars up from the caboose and he jumped for the back ladder and got snapped around between the cars. You couldn't feel nothing when he went under, but he sure was busted up when he come out." The man spoke apologetically. Sweat streaked his gray baggy railroad uniform.

Jesse looked down at his brother's body, sprawled brokenly over a desk in the station-master's office. A shattered arm protruded from a sleeve. Cinders and gravel pockmarked the skin. Legs twisted at odd angles. The face was battered into strangeness, no longer Ransome. Jesse turned away.

"Why'd he . . . the trailing ladder?" he asked, his voice catching.

"All I know is when I seen him he was stepping up the roadbed and then standing with his arms kind of stiff, like he didn't know what he was doing. I watched him till he jumped and got jerked around between the cars." Sweat crept down over the railroadman's face. He flicked a drop from his nose. "This come out of his shirt." He handed Jesse a soiled paper that was partly unfolded.

Jesse recognized it. "Thanks," he said, very quietly.

The railroadman would not look at Ransome's torn body, but he nodded towards it as he asked Jesse: "He coming to see you?"

"Yeah . . . yeah. I'm his brother." His voice died.

He stared again at his brother's young body, so strangely contorted on the desk-top. *That was Ransome. Ransome was in that. My brother left home and this has arrived.* Again his voice rose: "We were moving to Chicago. We were moving . . ."

Father and son loaded the coffin onto the pickup. Driving south, neither turned round to look at the long box on the bed of the truck, yet both were aware of the son and brother lying broken there, aware especially of the brokenness, as if he were something each had to put together again.

"Will you stay?" Morgan asked.

"Only long enough to bury him and help you with the planting."

"Then you're moving to Chicago?"

"Then I'm moving on to Chicago."

Their route into Mississippi carried them for barren miles between the railroad and the river. As the heat of the Mississippi day slowly gathered above the flat and boundless fields, the sun turned the rails into ribbons of silver, and burned even the muddy and turgid river into molten gold.

"Why do you have to go?" Morgan asked.

After a moment's pause, Jesse answered, "It's what Ransome and I were planning to do."

Morgan's voice burst inside the small cab of the truck, fierce and full of pain. "Ransome's dead!"

"You blaming *me* for that?"

"All I'm saying is, you cain't use him as an excuse for running away."

"You *are* blaming me. But he was running away from *you*."

"And who was he running away to see? You tell me that. His big brother up in Memphis? Big brother full of city talk, too good for farming, too good for living in the country. Hot for money and slick women and bright lights. You tell me what bait he was jumping for when he grabbed at that train!" Looking away from the road, Morgan glared at Jesse; but then, seeing his face, he relented. He lifted one fist from the wheel and uncurled the fingers, letting the hand fall on Jesse's knee. "And maybe it was me, too. There's been fathers easier to live with." He fell silent, one hand still on Jesse's knee, as if to lay claim to this one wandering son. Then he said, "Don't matter what we think or do, won't any of it bring him back."

As they rounded a curve, the coffin shifted in the truck bed, coming to rest against a bag of seed corn. Jesse forced himself to stare back through the rear window at the pine box. The few nails were only driven halfway in, because his mother would want a look. The grain of the wood was straight and clear. The handles on the side were of rope. The corners were mitered. Jesse tried reducing the coffin to a mere box, but it lodged in his brain, heavy and immovable. It was the first thing he had ever lifted that he knew he would never be able to put down. Delivered like a cruel present by the night train, Ransome lay in there, broken, a coded message that would take a lifetime to interpret.

Wake

Racing, the motorcycle fierce between his legs, black pavement tearing away beneath him, streetlights leaping at him, Lake Michigan on his right hand blurring as the motorcycle roared down a tunnel of darkness, and Herschel's voice behind him crying *Jesse slow down,* yet not hearing that voice or any living voice, only roaring ever faster between the city and the lake, looking for a wall to smash into, Herschel begging *Jesse for God's sake,* a brother waiting for him in that dark tunnel, the beach a glaze of sand, lake a glitter of stars, voice pleading, fierce speed gaining, darkness waiting darkness dark

The flashlight cast silhouettes of veins upon his retina. Jesse opened his eyes, winced, squeezed them shut. He let out a wail of pain.

"Easy now," a man's voice boomed. "Keep still."

"Where's my brother?" Jesse demanded feverishly.

"He's lying down right over there, and he's going to be all right. Just a few scrapes. You take it easy."

Jesse could hear moaning. His own lips trembling. "He's not hurt bad?"

"No, not bad. Now let's see if you can move your legs."

"You're lying. He's all busted up." Jesse panted. "He's going to die."

"He's not dying. You hit some gravel and skidded out, but your buddy's going to be just fine. A few stitches, a headache. So keep quiet now, and we'll have an ambulance here in a few minutes. Your foot, then — can you move your foot?"

"I didn't mean it, I swear I didn't. I wanted Ransome to live, more than anything. Don't listen to my father. He thinks I killed him."

"How about your arm?" the man said. "Can you lift an arm? No? All right, try to look at me. How many fingers am I holding up?"

Jesse could move nothing except his lips, could see no fingers, no hand. "You're lying to me. He's not alive . . . he's broken . . . the train . . ."

From nearby someone muttered groggily, "O my God, Jesse, what a mess. What the devil got into you, driving like that?"

Jesse could not make his head turn to look at this new voice. "Who's that?" he cried. "Ransome? He's not Ransome! Where's my brother?"

"Jesse, listen to me. It's Herschel."

Herschel? Then with a flare of anger he remembered — the gambling, the fight, the roar across Chicago on the motorcycle hunting for death. Herschel still alive — and Ransome truly dead. Stars of pain floated like great water-lilies in Jesse's mind. Then there was darkness. I am broken. Cover all but my hollow eyes and show me to my father.

In profile, Herschel looked for all the world like Ransome: the turned-up lady-killing mustache, wavy red hair, eye-sockets as hollow as a mule's, brows arched with a permanent question. The forehead that would be raked by gravel months later, after the motorcycle accident, was as smooth now as a pillow case, just as Ransome's had been. While Jesse watched, the eye-pits regarded themselves in the mirror, squinting:

"Do I look like an officer?" Herschel asked. "A suitable antagonist for the Japanese?"

Those were surely Ransome's eyes, his beard-shadowed chin and jaw. But the captain's uniform with its ironed creases, braid on the shoulders, patches on the chest — Ransome would never have worn such a get-up. "What you look like is a card-shark," Jesse replied.

"Shark is right, and I'm going out to Fort Collins and eat up all the little soldier fishes with their fresh paychecks. Won't we be grand, setting up in business on my earnings?"

"Greater miracles have been known to happen," said Jesse.

"O ye of little faith!" Herschel intoned, spitting on the toe of his shoe and gazing at himself in the shine. "Trust in me, and I will bring home the proverbial bacon."

For three months, ever since fleeing the break-my-back cotton fields of Mississippi and arriving at the Chicago bus station with a cardboard suitcase in each fist and meeting this slick-talker on the platform selling giveaway Bibles, Jesse had been trusting in Herschel. Even after months of working in a mattress factory to buy food and pay rent for both of them, while Herschel lolled about scheming of ways to make a fortune, Jesse still believed in him. Studying him now, Jesse felt that this primping peacock truly could be Ransome slicking on the brilliantine for Saturday night. "What do I tell Grace if she shows up?"

"Tell her I'm out making the great American fortune, to be used in founding the Great American Bedding Company, whose luxurious products will be constructed by Jesse Morgan and will be tested by her voluptuous self and me."

"I ain't repeating that," Jesse said.

"Then at least tell her to keep her hot little mitts off my redheaded roommate."

Herschel adjusted the cap, peered into the mirror, smoothed his face into sheeply innocence, then made for the door.

"Herschel, you want me to look through the obituaries, in case you lose all the money we got to buy supper with?"

The counterfeit captain pondered. "Perhaps so. A wise precaution. Make sure they say 'wake,' because that means food. The more Irish the better."

Watching Herschel leave, so tall and straight and pumped full of juice, Jesse remembered his brother alive, and then his brother dead: Ransome broken on the train-master's table, every inch of him covered except the tattered face. From the windowsill Jesse picked up his wood-carving and resumed work, whittling the tight-grained walnut in delicate shavings. Beyond the ledge another Chicago night

snarled and threatened. Towers spiked the air. Sirens filled the streets
with the wail of knifed hogs. To Jesse the city seemed poisoned with
lights; it was a wonder people could sleep. Below on the sidewalk
a trash barrel tipped over, booming in the brick canyons like artillery.

The shape of fingers emerged atom by atom from the walnut as
Jesse carved beside the window, on the lap of the evening, his eyes
occasionally daring sorties into the city beyond the ledge. *Wake,* he
thought, *wake.* And he remembered sitting all night over that abandoned husk of Ransome, only those hollow eyes still belonging to
his shattered brother, eyes not alive, eyes so dead they were merely
signs of him, prints Ransome had left behind in the mud of his flesh.
At a great distance Jesse's carving hands followed his mind, and his
mind followed his hands. Smoothing, smoothing, his fingers caressed
the wood.

"What are you making, Jesse?"

Startled, he looked up. Grace had entered with the quietness of
a grazing deer, and now stood watching him from an arm's length
away. "What are you making?" she repeated, unbuttoning her coat.

"Herschel's out."

"I can hear that. It's so quiet without his pontificating. But what
are you carving? The grain is lovely."

He balanced the dark wood on the windowsill, where it merged
into the dusky skyline of smokestacks and towers. Jesse dreaded
those towers, giants with neon signs blazing on their foreheads. Any
hour they might begin closing the circle to crush him. "They're supposed to be hands." He held up the lump of wood to show the palms
beginning to cup, the fingers stretching, the thumbs taking on defini-
tion.

"They look very strong. Like yours."

Not mine, he thought. Ransome's hands on the reins of the draft
horses, wrapped around a plow's handle, a fiddle-bow, a hammer.
Jesse's own fingers now smoothed the knife blade over a whetstone.
He kept his eyes from the woman, who stood at the center of the
room beneath the dangling bulb, her body a sun drawing him with
a fierce gravity that required all his will to resist. Her blouse parted
over shadows at the base of her throat. Her feet played nervously
under the hem of her skirt. I got to go somewhere, Jesse thought.

"They're grasping something," said Grace, stroking one of the wooden fingers. When Jesse refused to comment, she said, "So where's God's gift to women?"

"Playing cards at Fort Collins."

"*Cards?*" She stamped her foot furiously. "Jesse Morgan, you promised you wouldn't give him any more money for poker."

Speaking in a rush, not believing his own pell-mell words, Jesse said, "Well, he got it into his head, you see, how we were going to be partners at making beds and mattresses, same as I'm doing for Furman's now, only we'd own the outfit ourselves and get all the profit, and pretty soon get rich, buy us each a mansion, but to get us started he had to win a pile of money at poker on the army base, and before he could do that I had to give him a stake."

"I can't decide which of you is the more exasperating idiot." She huffed away, straightening the apartment in a fury.

Glancing at her warily as she washed the dishes, gathered tangles of socks, stacked the newspapers, Jesse felt every movement of her body within himself, his own center of gravity shifting in sympathy with hers. Herschel, he thought, if God hadn't made you the spitting image of my brother, I'd steal your woman and leave this filthy city.

Her sounds vibrated through his hands and left their mark on the wood he was carving. Her furious clatter echoed first in the kitchen, then in the bathroom, then in the bedroom. Finally Grace approached him once again and waited beneath the ceiling light, the silky womanly sounds of her body rustling near him.

"Jesse, are you angry?"

"What have I got to be mad about?"

"I don't know, but you haven't so much as looked straight at me since I came in."

Even when he turned, obeying the lure, he could only see the red of lips and fingernails, the deep dark burning red of her blouse and skirt. He was afraid to look directly into her face. She tugged nervously at her dimestore rings. At least here is some direction, he thought. Just yield and go to her.

"It's because of the other night," she said, hurt in her voice. "Hasn't any other woman ever asked you to sleep with her? Did I scare you?"

His hands gripped the knife for support. He shook his head doggedly. "Grace, I can't do that to Herschel." Although he would not look at her directly, he could feel the blouse rising and falling, a surf lapping against his raw nerves. He collected every walnut shaving into a shoebox, concentrating with great care on the task. He tested the blade's edge against his thumb before closing the knife. His hands felt lost.

She rustled closer. "Is he such a good friend? He's good at talking, I'll give him that. And at using people. I know all about it. But that doesn't make me his property." Her hand settled on his forearm like a leaf.

"Grace, I . . ."

"You haven't been teasing with me and making over me all these months just out of politeness."

As he tried to answer again, she put her fingers on his mouth. "Shush now," she whispered, opening her arms. Yielding to her gravity, he could make out no features, only the luminous red of her silhouette. Finding at least this direction in the city, he drew her close against him, as if her body and his own were two hands clasped.

Sitting on the floor with his sleeping head in her lap, she stroked his hair upon the furrowed meadow of her skirt. "Jesse, hey, it's late. Wake up."

The night reclaimed him slowly. Chicago glared in at every window, except the window framing a moon-glittered square of Lake Michigan. The lake you could not see across, which he had promised to show to Ransome.

Suddenly remembering, Jesse lurched upright, and said, "Where's Herschel?"

"Still out gambling, I guess."

"Did I go to sleep?"

She smiled down at him, peeling sweaty red curls from his forehead. "For two hours."

"You've just been sitting here all that time?"

"Watching the lake," she said, "and the lights. Everything's larger at night."

Jesse straightened his love-softened body, rubbing his eyes and fighting the sense of having betrayed his friend. "I've been a long time without touching anybody," he explained, apologizing. Ever since Ransome's funeral. Not a touch of his skin on another's in all those months.

She smoothed the furrows from her skirt, and pursed her lips as if to speak, but didn't, resting silent and cross-legged on the floor. Her blouse was buttoned and the stockings were drawn taut over her ankles. The ceiling light dazzled above her.

"He'd never forgive me if he found out," Jesse said.

"Who's going to tell him?"

Footsteps rattled in the stairwell, like loose seeds in a year-old gourd, and presently Herschel lunged into the room, holding aloft a fistful of greenbacks like a bouquet. "Gracie, my girl," he proclaimed, draping his arm over Jesse's shoulder, "you are looking at the Great American Bedding Company."

Mom, it's been a long time and I don't suppose you've heard any more about me than I've heard about you. Dad had no right blaming me for Ransome's death, or saying I deserted the farm. But I suppose he's found he can get by without me, and me without him. Anyway, if he won't read this, tell him I haven't starved, and I'm not in jail. Also tell him I've been a carpenter and lately a furniture-maker, which he taught me well. And there's no hunting in Chicago—except for people, and they shoot some of them most every day. I'm not in the army, and they won't get me in unless I go broke or crazy, or else if Hitler comes on over across the ocean. But what I wrote for was to tell you I set up with a buddy of mine and now I'm a manufacturer of beds and mattresses. The one thing people have to do is sleep, even during a war. We'll sell lots of them in Europe, because they're all busy making guns. When I come back to Mississippi I won't jump the train, I'll ride in my own Buick. You keep a lookout.

Jesse

"He supplies the hands and I supply the brains," Herschel declared.

The rasping shears halted abruptly, like crickets frightened, and Jesse looked up from the mattress fabric he was cutting, glancing first at Grace and then at Herschel. "I asked you not to say that," he said.

"The dignity of labor!" proclaimed Herschel, bowing humbly.

"Damn it, Herschel, you don't supply anything but money. I supply the hands *and* the brains. Left on your own you couldn't stuff a pillow, let alone make a bed or a mattress."

"My dear, you see the workers are restless," Herschel began, in a tone of ridicule that Jesse had heard once too many times.

"Get the hell out of here!" Jesse shouted, flashing and darting the shears as he waved at the door. "Go keep your books! Write down all those fat numbers!"

"Come along, Gracie," said Herschel. "We have offended our craftsman."

"You go ahead," she answered, never budging from the pile of cotton stuffing where she had assumed her customary strawboss position, legs nestled beneath her skirt. "I'll be along in a few minutes."

After Herschel departed with a mocking scowl, Jesse's shears resumed the circuit of the mattress pattern, beating their rounds, the stuff dividing on either side of the blades like the wake of a boat.

"You shouldn't pay attention to him," Grace observed soothingly.

He kept his head down and his mouth shut. Four thicknesses of cloth yielded to the shears, reproducing the pattern, adding to the pile of shaped cloth near the sewing machine. Tonight was the weekly cutting. Tomorrow and the next two days Jesse would sew; the day following he would stuff cotton into the mattress covers; the remaining three days he would cut and glue the maple beds. Then the night of that last day he would kneel again on this workroom floor and reduce the cloth to pattern. And that was the Great American Bedding Company.

"Jesse, you work too hard." Her legs stretched beneath the skirt, like cats begging a petting.

"I've got to make some money so I can leave Chicago and get a fresh start somewhere else," he said.

"But you can't do that overnight."

"It doesn't look like I'll ever do it. We sell dozens of these damn beds but we can't seem to make any money."

Her voice rose briefly above the rasp of the shears: "Don't you have a hunch why that is?"

"No, I sure don't. Ask Mister Herschel. He keeps the books."

She stood at the window with hands on hips, gazing down at the

curve of lights that divided the city from the lake. One side of the
boundary was intense with brightness, the other with darkness; but
even that other side had been invaded, the lights of docks and
freighters parceling out the night.

Without turning around she announced quietly, "Herschel finally
asked me to marry him."

The shears paused, and Jesse studied them intently, as if their stillness mystified him. He did not know what to answer.

"Well, don't you care?" Grace demanded.

"What do you want me to say?"

"Say anything. Say you'll carry me to Mississippi on your shoulders. Say you'll stuff him in a mattress. Tell me you love me and
you want me and you won't let him have me."

Beyond where she stood at the window Jesse could see the froth
of city lights spreading like galaxies on the velvety black void of the
lake. One gliding red light blinked rapidly, the pace of his heartbeat. How easy it would be to just go away with her, follow that
light, if only he could hate Herschel enough. He leaned back on his
heels, his arms aching from the shears, his head from the heat.
"Grace, you know how I feel."

"How?" she cried. "What am I to you? A lap when you're lonely?
Something soft to touch?"

Her back shook from sobs, yet he did not trust himself to reach
out for her. The heat clogged his mind; he could not think what to
do, to say. Tell her yes, Grace, I need you? Let's run off together
away back south? No, no, he couldn't betray another brother. He
picked up the shears and tested their bite with two sharp snaps at
the cloth.

"Jesse!" She spun away from the window, hissing his name, her
neck drawn taut, her fists clenched and eyes swollen. "Make up your
mind!"

With a great effort, as if shoving a mud-stuck wagon, he said,
"I won't steal women from my friends."

She fixed him with a red-eyed glare, saying fiercely, "He doesn't
own me."

"It's just that me and Herschel are buddies. Partners."

"Some partners! You get the calluses while he gets the profits."

"We both get the profits."

"Don't be too sure about that."

He looked at her sharply. "What do you mean?"

Grace collapsed onto the mound of cotton, tearing off wads and rolling them into balls and throwing them out the window.

"What do you mean?" Jesse demanded.

"You don't belong in Chicago," she said, yanking out a fistful of the cotton. "You're just an overgrown backwoods kid."

"Don't throw that stuffing out the window. It costs money."

"You're a redneck and a hick and a fool!" she cried. "I'd give him up for you, but I can't give up both."

He tried to hold back the words, but they came anyway: "Then you'd better go on ahead and marry your city man."

Dear Mom,

No, they haven't drafted me yet. But ever since Pearl Harbor they've been hunting up every able-bodied man they can find. I know how you and Dad feel about soldiering, and I feel the same. Why don't you say anything about Dad when you write? He's got to accept that I'm grown up and in business for myself. My partner has got married to a beautiful girl up here. I wish she had a sister. But there's no chance me getting married until I can see a little further ahead where I'm walking. I might come home for a visit over Christmas. What would you and Dad think about that? I'd have to take the train this time, on account of the war makes cars hard to come by. Write and let me know if he wants me to come home. Tell him I make my beds sound and proper.

Jesse

All Jesse could think to do on their wedding night was roar through Chicago on his motorcycle, ignoring stop lights, swerving between the delivery trucks and late trolleys. No matter where he drove, streets sliced across his path. At every intersection he slowed down, bewildered, needing to go on but not knowing where. The labyrinth of bricks and concrete dared him to choose a direction.

When he could put it off no longer, on the morning after the wedding, Jesse trudged up to the workloft. He knocked, waited, knocked again. He thought he could hear, through the closed door, the sound of their bodies untwining in a slither of sheets. Grace admitted him, eyes elusive, then fled into the kitchen trailing wisps of nightgown, altogether so soft and filmy that the racket she soon made among the pans seemed incredible.

"Jesse, my man," declared Herschel, who sprawled in a snarl of pillows and sheets, "you sure make one wicked hell of a bed."

"Look, Herschel, it was your idea to sleep here in the shop."

"Don't you worry about us old married folks." Herschel slapped his bare stomach and rooted among the pillows for a discarded pajama bottom. "Last night wasn't the first time by a long sight. It was just the first legal time." He raised his voice. "That right, Gracie?"

The kitchen roared with pans and spoons.

"Look," Jesse said, stooping over a wooden bed frame that he had nearly completed the afternoon before, "I don't think this is going to work, you two living here and me coming and going."

"Of course it will work! You just keep making beds, Jesse boy, and I'll sell them, and Gracie and I'll use them."

"Maybe she doesn't like me barging in here and you talking like that."

"I'll worry about what my little woman likes and doesn't like." Laden with fresh clothes, Herschel proceeded to the bathroom. "Jesse?"

He allowed himself to look up. Only her face showed around the edge of the kitchen door, and it seemed the same face. He had hoped the wedding and loving would alter it, weaken its appeal. But desire for her still seized him like a fist.

"Coffee and toast?" she asked, with a forced gaiety.

"Sure. That would be dandy."

Her hair disappeared last, like the flicker of a deer's tail extinguishing itself in forest. After nearly gluing a brace in upside down, Jesse paused to calm himself, thinking, *O Lord I got to get out but where tell me where.*

Presently, she served the plate of toast and mug of coffee, setting them on the floor at his side. The flow of her body cut channels through the air, and through his nerves: bending to touch the floor, then hovering before him, hands on hips, head tilted to one side.

"Sorry it's a little burnt on the edges," she said.

Stuffing a triangular wad of jellied toast in his mouth, Jesse mumbled, "No, no, it's fine. Just the way I like it."

She watched him intently while he ate, until he grew ashamed. He gripped the mug in both hands and turned away from her to sip the coffee. Laughing, she said, "You eat here anytime you want!" then set about straightening the bed, sweeping cotton back onto its white mound, picking up Herschel's underwear. With every movement she made, he felt that sympathetic shifting deep within himself. Every one of her gestures—serving the coffee, calling out the window to birds, scrubbing the breakfast dishes—stirred him now as the ceremonial gestures of ministers had stirred him when he was a boy. But they also moved him as the spring moved him, and it was this deeper motion that he feared.

Go where? he thought, the coffee scalding his lips. *Home to red-dirt Mississippi? And wouldn't that be defeat? Back to Dad like a dog with my tail between my legs. And if not the farm, then maybe the war?*

Herschel reappeared amid steam from the shower, damp hair clinging to his head like the cap on a mushroom. "Man was created to make love, sleep, take a hot shower, and make love. This man in particular."

"Herschel—" Jesse began.

"You know, my friend, you really ought to get married."

"Herschel—"

"Then that ugly face of yours wouldn't always hang down like a horse's muzzle."

"I'm trying to tell you—"

"On the other hand," Herschel continued, "that would reduce the amount of energy you have left over for work, and that would diminish the profits, and that—I don't need to remind you—would be bad all around."

"Herschel, I'm quitting," Jesse said firmly. "I'm through. Not another damn bed. Not another day in this room."

The mocking grin quickly faded. "You're kidding."

"I'm dead serious. I want out, and right away. I can't stand any more of this."

A look of panic swept over Herschel's face. "Grace!" he yelled. "Come in here!"

She hurried in carrying a dish towel. The gown hillocked over her breasts and draped about her ankles. Jesse remembered licking salt from those ankles. "What on earth's the matter?"

"He wants to break up the partnership."

"Why ever for?" she asked.

Jesse squatted on the floor holding two pieces of a bed frame. How did they fit together? He thought of the pale, sunless skin on the undersides of her breasts.

"Now, Gracie," said Herschel, retreating into the kitchen, "you explain to this moody man that if he stops making beds and mattresses for so much as one week, we are all in the gutter, and one or two of us may be in jail."

When Herschel was beyond earshot, she stooped over Jesse and spoke as to a child, in the voice she used for coaxing the sparrows that braved the grimy window ledge. "What is it?"

She enveloped him, her scent, her gown lolling, her warmth radiating like the return of feeling to a numbed hand.

"I'm just sick of Chicago, fed up with this work, and I want to go away. Is that so hard to figure out?" He was afraid to look at her, afraid of what his eyes would reveal. The bed frame suddenly made no sense, bits of wood sprawled without pattern on the floor.

"It's something else," she insisted. "What is it? What?" She took him by the shoulders. There was no place left for his eyes to settle, except on her face. "Is it me?" she almost pleaded. His head nodded forward, not assent but simply a yielding, and she beseeched him, "O, Jesse, is it me?"

Jesse did not want to believe her when she told him that Herschel had lost all their earnings, gambled them away, any more than he had wanted to believe his own suspicions for weeks past.

"What he didn't lose at cards," Grace explained, her voice sinking, "he spent on women. It seems he never can get enough of women."

Jesse's arms ached from wanting to smash something. His hands lay helpless on his knees. What he felt was worse than anger, was utter loss, betrayal. "We were like brothers."

"That's where you were wrong," she told him gently.

"He lied to me from one end to the other. From the day I met him."

"Jesse, I'm sorry. What could I do? I tried to warn you."

He could hear the tears rising, like the waters at a mud dam in his father's pasture, but he ignored the sound. "Sorry doesn't undo a thing. It won't bring a soul back." He withdrew completely from the room, from the night, lapsing back half a year until he stood again on that station platform in Memphis, waiting for the last train from Mississippi. Overwhelmed by the memory, he spoke aloud in a furious voice: "I went to meet him and we were fixing to come up here to Chicago. He was going to shag a train, you know, the way I always did. Only he didn't know how, the fool kid, and he lost hold and fell under the wheels and all they delivered on that train was a busted-up body that didn't even look much like Ransome. Except for those mule's eyes, it could have been anybody."

"Who on earth are you talking about?" Grace asked.

"My brother, dammit, my brother! Who do you think? He was running from the farm and from my old man, the same as me. He jumped at a train to come join me, big brother in the city, but the train didn't stop except to pick up that fool broken kid and carry him on to me. We were coming up here to have us a time, you see, maybe start us a business, make us some money, become somebody, so we could go back home and prove to our folks that we were free of that land, free of that life. We were going to do it together. We were going to be . . ." His voice was cut short by the anger in his throat. He raised his fists in the air. "Free of all that."

"So you tried making all that happen with Herschel? Taking him for your brother?"

"I tried it. But that's done now. Gone."

Grace laid a palm against his cheek. "Not everything's gone. Herschel swears he can get some of the money back. Enough to pay the bills."

"I wouldn't care now if he hauled it in here on a wheelbarrow. I trusted him. I built everything in this city around that man."

"He said, if you'd drive him across town on your motorcycle, there are some girls . . ." Grace paused. "There are some things they have that he can sell."

"The way I'm feeling, he hadn't better get on any motorcycle with me." Jesse set about gathering his tools. Those, he owned.

"I'm still here," she said close to his ear.

His own pain deafened him to the pain in her voice. He fitted the chisels into their canvas sack. With a rag he smeared oil on the blade of the miter saw. Finally missing the sound of her, he turned, but she was gone. The mound of cotton had spread its avalanche across the pathway. Maple planks waited uncut against the wall. Mattress covers, lacking stuffing, seemed in need of breath to give them shape. All the room waited for him. The fragments cried for hands to assemble them, but his own hands were shaking.

One brother shattered beneath a train, one brother betrayed him, one woman fled. He was a moon without a planet, wobbling in a crazy orbit about a vacuum.

Beyond the window Chicago lost its nightly shoving match with the lake, the lights of the city gradually dissolving in the crescent of darkness. And that crescent was only the border of a vast sphere of darkness. If you looked away from the lights altogether, the blackness, the absence of city, the vast fields of nothingness stretched further than you could see, clear to the end of the universe. It was enough to put a man in a rage, all that darkness to get through before you reached the other side, if there was another side.

Mom,

Don't you worry. The motorcycle was all tore up. But I only got scraped up some and my head banged. I was several kinds of fool to go riding around when I was feeling so low and mean. Anyway, I got worse news. I didn't tell you sooner because I figured you had enough to fret over already. The bed-and-mattress business went broke—never mind how. And when I started looking for another job, the army roped me in, gave me some tests, and here I am in a uniform, waiting to ship out in the morning for the Pacific. They made me a sniper—that's what all that hunting with Dad did for me. At camp they had me aiming at these targets shaped like a man, and it turned my stomach. Lord knows how I'll feel when I see the real thing. I'm just not made for killing.

I send a box of my things. There's another one at Mrs. Tibbett's in Memphis, that red sea chest, which maybe you would write to ask for, because I am short of time. If Dad gets the warden's job at the prison, will there be a place in the house for me? I don't know where else to go after this war. Everything seems closed in, and there's no one up here in Chicago but me. I better quit this now. Everybody is packing. I'll write from over there, across the water. Tell Dad — no, never mind.

                                                                    Jesse

Skeletons rattled among the sugarcane. Tracking them at dusk he would find their spidery footprints in the loam of the fields, and in the red dirt of the roads. He knew their shattered bodies were moldering beneath the house, within the furrows of the cotton fields, along the gravel banks of the Mississippi River, at the bottom of the prison wells. And he knew that when their bones had become as clean as the peeled branches of a willow tree, they would rattle among the sugarcane, they would clatter at night upon the ceiling, they would wind the sheets around his body until nothing showed but the eyes. To guard against them, every night he kept watch until the steady leaching of the darkness toward daylight forced him to sleep.

"Jesse, do you want some lemonade?" said his mother.

"No, ma'am," he answered.

"Are you feeling all right?"

"Yes, ma'am."

"Is that chair comfortable?"

He lunged forward and then reared backward in the rocking chair, but quietly, quietly. "It's fine, ma'am, fine."

"Don't you want to come inside out of the heat and lay down a while? You know what the doctor said."

"Yes, ma'am."

"Well, then, come on along."

Jesse followed the lumbering shape of his mother over the loose boards of the porch, which he trod gingerly, for fear of the noise. Her footsteps deafened him; her bare feet, horny on the soles, rasped over the wood like feedsacks dragging.

"Lie you down. Let me take off your shoes. Now you don't need those sheets up around you like that. Let go, honey."

"I need them." He twisted his hands into the sheet and would not yield.

"All right, all right. Just lie still a spell, and try to rest." Her hand smoothed the sweat from his forehead, the hand dusty with flour, while her other hand tracked the stray hairs that had escaped her pins.

"What'll I think about?"

"Think about the river," she said. "Think about the cotton growing, about the birds flying."

Terror gripped him as his mother shuffled away. "Mother, close the door."

"Honey, there'll be no breeze."

"Please shut it. To keep things out."

"Well, you call if you get troubled." She drew the door closed behind her.

At the sound of the five o'clock shotgun, the prisoners in the fields, who were bent double over their hoeing, straightened threateningly, like jackknives opening. Jesse's hands whitened on the arms of his rocking chair. His mother, standing behind, rested his head against her stomach.

"It's over now, honey," she said. "Just you relax."

"I didn't want to shoot," he said, for the hundredth time.

"I know, child, I know. We none of us wanted the killing. Put it out of your mind." Her voice rocked him, as her hands rocked him in the chair.

The open jackknives gathered at the edge of the cotton field, one hundred blades glistening, the bayonets of a small army, under the keeping of a white man whose shotgun gleamed and flared in the sunset.

"I aimed at them and they fell," he said, his head shaking. "I didn't want that." His eyes widened, staring, refusing to blink, his arms lifting, his head inclining to one side. "You put the cross-hairs on their heart, you move your finger just a tiny bit, and poof! they're gone." His head jerked from side to side as if someone were slapping him. "O God, no! No!"

"Quiet, child, quiet yourself," her voice almost singing now, and then actually singing, a song without words, only the sound running over him, soothing him, allowing him to open his eyes. Her vast body seemed to surround him. The tiny flowers on her dress cast their scent about him.

The army of black convicts formed into columns under the eyes of their white general, whose lifted gun-barrel flamed in the sunset. Jesse could not hear their feet, but he could see the trail of red dust they left in their wake, as they marched in slow time from the fields to the barracks, the troops of the dead.

"Is it Dad?" Jesse asked, skewing his head backwards to look at his mother, but pointing at the white general.

"Yes, that's Dad," she answered.

"He wouldn't shoot. Dad wouldn't."

"He's never had to, Jesse, thank the Lord."

"He doesn't ask about me, does he?"

"O yes he does, child, yes he does. He's always wanting to know how you're feeling, when you'll get well."

"I don't think I'll ever get over the war."

"Yes you will, sweetheart. You surely will."

Without sound from the bare feet tramping in the dust, the troop of black convicts filed before the warden's house, where Jesse sat on the porch to pass them in review.

"Has anybody won the war yet?" he asked.

"Not yet," she answered. "But they say we're ahead."

"Ahead!" He spat beyond the porch railing. "The ones that don't die will be coming home, and then we'll see how far ahead we are."

The woman's voice crackled in the telephone. It seemed remote and minuscule, as if it were echoing down a long tunnel. He had to strain to make out what she was saying.

"Jesse," came the tiny voice, "it's Grace. What's wrong with you? Are you sick? Your mother didn't want me to talk with you. But this is an emergency. Jesse? Jesse?"

"Yes," he said.

"Are you sick? Don't you remember me? It's *Grace.* From Chicago. I need your help."

"I am afraid I am not well," he said carefully.

"What is it?" Static crackled in the tunnel through which she spoke. "I said, what's wrong?"

"The war, the . . . ," his voice falling. The effort of projecting sounds through that tunnel was too great.

"Well, Jesse, pull yourself together, because you've got to come up here. We need you. Herschel collapsed one day last week—Tuesday—and they had to operate on his spine, to remove some fluid, because there was so much pressure on his brain. And when he woke up . . . Jesse? Are you listening?"

"Yes."

"And when he woke up he asked for you. He said, 'Where's Jesse? Is Jesse all right?' He kept asking and asking about you. They had to hold him down. The last thing he could remember was the motorcycle accident, and he kept shouting, 'You got to help Jesse—please—somebody—he's hurt.' They stopped his raving, but he doesn't remember anything since the accident—and he doesn't remember much from before. The doctors say he must have had a blood clot. All he asks about is you. Jesse?"

"I'm here," he replied.

"Jesse," she said, her voice so thin that any wind in the tunnel would surely snap it, a piano wire stretched taut and vibrating at a painful pitch, "he doesn't remember me and he doesn't remember the baby. He won't even talk to me. He keeps saying, 'I didn't want to cheat him.' " Just when the fragile voice seemed broken at last, it sounded again faintly. "Jesse, please come. He's lost, his mind wanders all over creation, and all he lights on is you. Please come—please, please. We both need you."

"Where are you?" he said.

"I told you. We're in Chicago."

"That's a long way," he said.

"He's lost. He's all in bits and pieces. We need you." Static cavorted in the tunnel.

"I'll come," he said.

"What?" she shouted. "I can't hear you."

"I said, I'll come."

Walking to Sleep

The man in Georgia waking among pines
Should be pine-spokesman.
> —Wallace Stevens

Ivory bones of convicts still washed in spring rains from the hill where they had been buried, to driftwood the riverbank until the warden's men, with baskets and shovels, gathered them again. Polished as they wormed through the hill, they gleamed like peeled branches. The riverbank must be innocent of bones, for on summer evenings the warden would promenade there with his little granddaughter, who asked about every stone and stick, her petticoats hissing against the timothy grass, while beyond the burial hill convicts would still be chopping cotton, and the guards, nursing their rifles, would shade their eyes from the sunset.

Every convict who died on the prison farm, unless he were claimed by kin, was buried in Skeleton Hill. Convicts died for sundry reasons—too little food, too much work, talking back to guards, old age. Many men, it was said, had escaped during the twelve decades since the prison was opened. At any rate, many names in the register had been crossed through, bearing the legend VANISHED.

Old Monk, having served time in the prison longer than had any barn or tractor on the place, knew more of those vanished convicts than any other man. They had saddened him, every one, by their parting. On a morning, one of the white guards would swagger into the barracks with his shotgun and announce that Jeb or Lucius or Ezekiel had run off and no one could find a trace of him; but later Monk would sneak a visit to Skeleton Hill, and often he discovered there a new turning of earth. It made a man keep his peace, if he wanted to grow old.

Crickets in the parched grass seemed to rasp in time with the creaking of the porch swing, where the warden and the state superintendent of prisons sat talking, their legs lolling back and forth with just enough strength to keep the swing in fitful motion, as the rain that promised to quench the grass shimmered in its advance over the prison farm fields.

Seeing the warden's gray eyes drift out of focus, like the blur and scatter of rising smoke, the superintendent harshly repeated his question: "How you gonna keep them from running off?"

"Fear," the warden answered.

"Fear of what? Listen, Morgan, the governor won't take that for an answer. He's nervous as hell about the primaries. With the war shutting down he'll have a flood of niggers and white boys to find jobs for. Trouble in the prisons could swing the elections."

"Fear of each other," the warden explained. His work-hardened body tensed like a spring. "Fear will hold this place together like magnetism. None of my men trusts any other one further than he can throw him, and that's the way I aim to keep it."

"Because," the superintendent added, "the first time they take it into their heads to cooperate, you'll lose every damn prisoner you've got."

The warden's gaze crept over the horizon, pausing momentarily where the jackknifed figures of convicts bent over their work in the fields, each silhouette etched in isolation against the skyline. "They won't cooperate."

"You're absolutely sure of that?"

"Sure as I'm sitting here," the warden answered. He was tired of arguing with this man, who was just the governor's arm-twister and jaw-boner, a coward who'd rather shoot the convicts than let one man escape. Shifting his plug of tobacco from one cheek to the other, the warden spat towards a brown corner of the porch.

In the fields, the jackknifed figures straightened, and the prisoners, huddled between their guards, like circus animals parading between trainers, shambled toward their barracks.

Watching the clump of men advance in pace with the rain clouds over the field, the superintendent observed: "If they ever turn mean, they'll kill you and every white person on the place. Which includes your wife and that granddaughter."

"That's my lookout." The warden struggled against his fury.

"If a single man escapes—especially now as everyone's worried about all these nigger soldiers coming back from the war—the governor will pack you off before the ink's dry on the newspaper."

"You'd rather I do like my predecessors—and bury all the trouble-makers up on the hill under moonlight? If I was to invite some reporters in here to dig around in the books and in that hill—you know what they'd find?"

The superintendent's lips whitened. "Never you mind about the past."

"Well, then, there's your choice. You just shoot people, like all those white guards used to do. Or else you build a wall around this place and you hire soldiers with machine guns, and you patrol with dogs and put up some barbed wire—like that German bastard did with the Jews—"

"That's enough, Morgan."

"Or," the warden continued, "you do what I'm doing, and have the prisoners guard each other. You give the lifers guns, make sure there's always at least three in one place, then you set them to guard their buddies. Anyone who tries to escape gets shot. Whoever does the shooting gets set free."

The sullen group of convicts trudged by the porch. Where the warden saw one hundred forty-seven individual men, each with distinct gait, build, voice, the superintendent could only see one sinister animal, amoeboid in its undulating movement. For him all the separate bodies blended into one lump of black skin and rags, all the legs seemed to scramble beneath a single monstrous carcass. "You're crazy," watching the great beast squeeze into the whitewashed barracks, "you should have stuck to cotton-farming and told the governor to just pay you back in money for your campaign help."

"You go on home and worry about you," the warden said. "I'll worry about me and mine."

"Monk!" the warden's wife called from the kitchen behind the brick house. "You, Monk, come up here!"

"Yessum, yessum, just comin'." The old man shuffled the twenty steps from the wash shed to the kitchen, counting out the twenty paces as he walked. He carried his head forward, paying close attention to the earth immediately in front of his shoes. The steps to the kitchen he mounted painfully, with the care of an old man unsure of his footing or eyesight. Although he bore little flesh on his emaciated frame, he seemed to push against some great inertia. On the doorsill he kicked dust from his shoes, then opened the screen door and walked into the odor of sausages and biscuits.

Mrs. Morgan, red from the cooking, a woman built heavily by nature but swollen into lumbering shapelessness by years of cooking for men with the appetites of farmers, her white hair tucked back into a bun, wiped her hands on an apron as she turned to the old man.

"Are the baby's dresses washed?"

"Yessum," Monk said.

"Scrubbed good and white?"

"Yessum," standing out of the doorway as he spoke, and pointing towards the washyard where the granddaughter's dresses flapped upon the clothes-line. This earned a hum of approval from Mrs. Morgan.

Her hands emerged from the apron, raw about the knuckles. "And have you fetched the mail yet?" she asked him, kindly, as one who had reminded children and servants of small things for forty years, in a voice which was dwarfed by her body.

"No'm," he answered. He shook his head and smiled, his teeth yellow and ill-fitting. "This old man forgetting everything lately. Plumb slipped my mind."

She watched him amble towards the country road, at that pace so cumbrously slow that she wondered how he ever returned to the house. *Abe's going to have to get us a replacement nigger pretty soon*

because this poor lost old Monk's about wore out. From the stoop
she surveyed the canefields, gauged the weather, comparing it all
with the almanac, and then returned to the biscuits and sausages.

Monk's daily path carried him around the border of Skeleton Hill.
"Morning, gentlemen," he said as he touched the brim of his straw
hat, nodding at the mound of old graves. As always, when he
hobbled up the lane that led beyond the county road to the pasture,
and beyond that to the canefield, he thought of walking on and on.
He longed to pass the rusted mailbox where the errand for some
reason made him stop, as if his steps were measured out for him.
Six hundred eighty-three. Two more than yesterday, five more than
the day before. Yet he got no farther, and there was somewhere
beyond that he wanted to reach, but he had long since forgotten
where. There was always this last point — this mailbox mounted on
loops of welded chain, like a striking snake arrested in mid-air — at
which he had to turn and walk back towards the two-story house
where the warden lived with his wife, his youngest son, the son's
wife, and their little girl.

Dust rose around him in red puffs with every sluggish step. All
the weeds on both sides of the lane were powdered with it, his breath
was gritty with it, his muddy brown eyes — glazed with age and sun —
were stung by it. "Miss's dresses gonna be dirty already," he told
himself.

Having opened the mailbox and pawed out what letters or circulars
there were, he crossed the gravel road to the pasture. For a long time
he leaned against the barbed-wire fence and stared out across the
field, beyond the horses muzzling about for grass, and deep into the
wavering shades of the canebreak. The day had not yet touched the
heart of the cane. There, hidden in the intricate shades, the earth
was still cool. Monk could almost see the shadows wither as the sun
rose, shadows which at midday would be only fitful dancing spots
beside the stalks, and he was thinking, *Like the pines of Louisiana.*

"Here, babe," he called to the horses. They recognized him, twitching their rabbity ears, and began plodding toward the fence. He
scrabbled around in his pouch for loose scraps of tobacco. "Here
you be," he called familiarly, "this'll get rid of them worms." He
held out a long, bony hand with the shreds of tobacco in its yellow

palm. Their ears tilted forward in sign of trust, even when he ran his fingers over their muzzles to brush away the dirt, and with their black sandpaper tongues they licked his outstretched palm. Using his free hand he picked the gnats from their watery eyes.

Leaving them, he said, "Now you look after yourselves in this here heat. It's gonna be a hot one today."

Then he turned and trudged the dusty lane back to the house, the mail under one arm.

"Anything from your boy, Monk?" the warden's granddaughter asked, as she scampered from the porch to meet him.

"Nope, ain't nothing come today," he answered. The son had been lost, too, like everything else, in that continent of the past which had been cut free of the present and drifted forever out of reach—a past no longer in time at all, but only in the woolly memory of the old man. That son now lingered only as a name to search for on letters, no longer as a face to recall, no longer as a voice or body.

"Well, Miss Fay," he said, "and how be you this fine morning?" The girl caught his hand and held it by the little finger. A giggle and a skip was all she answered, flipping her petticoat with every playful jerk of her knee. This morning she was a pony.

The name of the lost son rattled around in Monk's head, like a seed in a dried gourd, as he shuffled back to the wash shed. In one corner a gray pile of prison uniforms stank of men and sun. "Miss Fay, you best get you back up to the house, before your daddy fuss at you for talking with the old nigger-man."

"He don't fuss, Monk," she said, hopping first on one foot and then on the other around the washtub.

"Well somebody fuss."

"It's that snot Kirkus."

"Yeah, it would be Mastuh Kirkus," he said. "Well if you stay, you got to help." And she helped, by carrying him the bed sheets, one by one, dragging them over the damp wood floor. He resumed the rhythm of scrubbing, wringing and hanging with those lean arms whose muscles twisted like rope beneath the skin. As he worked he mumbled and hummed broken bits of song to himself.

"What you singing, Monk?" Fay asked.

"You don't like Monk's singing, missy?"

"It's all right. But what is it?"

"Why, it's . . ." Monk began, standing erect with both sinewy arms in the wash-tub, "it's . . . it's . . . I done forgot what it is."

"You forget a lot."

"Yes, missy."

"Kirkus says you're off in the head." He continued his scrubbing as she pranced around the shed, lifting her knees like a circus horse. "He says, 'That old buzzard's off in the head.' And he says my daddy's nuts on account of the war and all. But then Papaw, he lights into Kirkus and tells him to shut up. Just like that." She clacked her jaws together, like a trap snapping shut. "Nutty buzzard, nutty buzzard!" she cried, flapping her arms like the old bird she imagined. Suddenly she stopped. "And Kirkus says you killed a man. Killed a white man. Is that so?"

Monk paused in the scrubbing and tried his hardest to remember if that was so. There was a pine forest. There was a foreman at the lumberyard where he worked in the pine forest. In the forest there was a bed of dried needles. And on that bed — he was on that bed — with a woman. He was on that woman and it was good, goddamn good on that woman. Then there was the foreman with his boot on Monk's back, then with his boot on the woman's belly, and Monk was rolling on the ground with his ribs kicked in. Then there was the foreman grabbing at his woman. And there was a pine limb in Monk's hand. And there was a man with a crushed skull.

"It was a long time ago, child."

"Was it a white man?" she said.

"There were these pines, missy, you should have seen those pines. They were so old and soft. A man could lie there in the cool, breeze whisperin' up above, and them needles underneath you like a feather tick . . ."

Miss Fay stamped her foot. "I didn't ask about no pines!"

Yes, and on that woman was a ride for a man, even if it was the last ride. A man's hands leathered from the lumbering, but on that woman they were velvet again. A man became as tall and sinewy and proud as those pines.

"Monk, Monk!" Fay squealed, tugging at his arm. "Tell me!"

"O Lord," he said, whistling between his teeth. "Monk done forgot the mail. Look here, help this old man and carry this here bundle up to your mammy, honey." He fastened her tiny fingers around the letters and faced her towards the house, but she stamped her foot and would not move. "Mo-onk," she whined.

"Fay!" Mrs. Morgan shouted. "You, Fay? Come up here. And don't you get a spot on that dress."

"Get you gone," Monk said, and patted the girl's rump.

Fay hesitated.

"You, Fay!"

And then she ran.

"Do you have to clean that blame thing out here?" the warden demanded of his overseer.

Kirkus looked up from his shotgun at the warden, and then at Jesse, who was squatting on the porch steps, his chin on his hands, fidgety, staring into dusk.

"Jesse don't like my gun?" Kirkus said. "And why don't Jesse like my little gun?"

"What's in the newspaper tonight, Abe?" Mrs. Morgan said. She faced her husband, who sat in the porch swing, and she herself swayed back and forth in her rocker, stitching for a time on a feed-sack dress (which her granddaughter would pretend was satin), pausing every few moments to cool her face with a paper fan.

"Lies," Morgan said. "I don't know who're the bigger liars—the politicians in Jackson or the politicians in Washington. But it looks like they really mean to end the war this time."

At the mention of "war" Jesse's head jerked around. When his father refused to say any more, he rested his chin once again on his knees and stared into the dark.

The crickets rivaled the porch swing, rasping, the locusts sang in the tupelo trees, and Kirkus polished the barrels of his shotgun till they shone. Casually he said:

"You find you a job yet, Jesse?"

"Now don't you start in on him tonight," Mrs. Morgan said. "He'll be ready when he's ready."

Jesse glanced at his mother. Each swing of her fan sliced the moon in half.

As the warden's family sat around waiting for dinner to settle, they heard (between the rusty grinding of the porch swing and the harsh song of the locusts) Monk's gravelly voice, low, confidential, talking in the dark to the horses.

"Been working hard today, babe? Been dragging that sugar wagon? Get them flies off your nose and them gnats outen your eyes and you'll feel some better. That's a good baby, now, good baby. Monk ain't got no tobacca tonight. Have to do with the salt of these hands . . ."

The words hovered, separate, mysterious, out of the dark. They came from such a great distance that the night seemed fathomless. Snorts and whinnies from the horses blended with the old man's voice. Occasionally the horses' metal shoes clacked against stones in the pasture.

"Why don't that old black ghost quit spooking the horses and get inside like all the rest of the prisoners?" Kirkus said. "Gallivantin' round the place like he owned it. The old warden wouldn't have put up with it."

He jammed the cleaning rod down into the gun, jerked it out again.

"You're gonna wear that barrel out, you keep cleaning at it," the warden said.

"And now you're gonna let that nigger-man sleep next to your granddaughter. I swear you're a nigger-lover."

"You just keep on talking like that, Kirkus, and I don't care how many friends you got in Jackson, I'll turn your ass out," the warden said. The newspaper crackled like fire as he folded it and ran his fingers along the crease.

Jesse was soothed by Monk's cajoling voice, and by the horses' answering snorts. The hooves scraped and thudded on the dry hard earth. He listened to the faint rattle of the sugarcane where he knew the moths would be flirting, away beyond the county road, away over the pasture, at the very edge of moonlight. The moths hung peacefully from the sharp flat leaves. Peacefully. The war may have ended in Europe and might be near its close in Japan, but it continued to rage within Jesse, who had survived one year as a sniper in the Pacific jungles and had returned, discarded by the army, a man haunted by his victims, to family in Mississippi.

"They're looking to hire veterans," Kirkus said, returning to the sore spot, like a boy hammering at the bruise on his playmate's arm.

"Shut up," the warden said.

Jesse's wife, Marsha, crossed the porch from the house, paused to rest her hand on Jesse's head, then walked off into the dusk to take the evening walk her doctor had advised her to take. "Fay's asleep," she said as she passed. What slight breeze there was drew the gown taut over her mounded belly, as she drifted like a ferry-boat into the moonlight.

"After all, Jesse," Kirkus persisted, "you got a redheaded little girl and another kid on the way. They can't live off your daddy forever . . ."

"I said shut up," the warden repeated.

"You could hire on as a professional hunter . . ."

Jesse leaped at him, tumbled him against the porch wall, and began pounding his head on the floor — his mother howling, his father shouting — then he suddenly grew sick of it, he had killed too many men already, and so he let the stunned head fall and he fled, first walking and then running, until he disappeared down the lane.

"Kirkus," the warden said, "go see the barracks are locked." The overseer sat up in a daze, fumbling with the parts of his dismantled gun, which he intended to bear with him. "Git!" the warden ordered. And the overseer obeyed.

"He'll never get well with that devil around to torment him," Mrs. Morgan said.

"He's got too many relatives in office to fire him. Besides, there won't anybody else take his job," her husband answered.

"Maybe one of these boys when they come back from the war?" she suggested.

"No. They'd be worse killers than him, and there's already been too much killing on this place." He glanced toward Skeleton Hill, a hump in the moonlight.

Monk neared the porch, singing odd snatches from his ragbag of half-remembered songs.

"You, Monk," Mrs. Morgan said. "You hush."

"The baby asleep?" he said.

"Yes. And now you go in to her quiet."

"Yessum," he replied, and padded silently into the house. Nights he slept on a litter next to the granddaughter's crib, where he had slept since her birth four years before, where he had slept with the children and grandchildren of eight different wardens, and in the still darkness of the nursery he rambled over his old stories. Now with this last child he was a child himself. His eyes danced with hers — his own eyes which were normally so tired and sunken, with almost no border any more between the brown irises and the muddy whites. In the dark, sitting on the bedside and listening to his own voice, Monk would stare and stare through the window-screens into the rustling, cricket-filled night, and see that former world of pines bending in the wind, would smell pitch, hear the pad of rain on needles. When thunderstorms beat through the canefields, he thought he really heard his pines again, resisting the wind and water. Then he would put that skinny finger to his lips, whisper "Shush!" and Fay would squeeze herself into a ball beneath the sheets, her eyes and mouth gaping, waiting in frightened silence for the old man to finish his story.

On the porch the warden and his wife waited for their son to return. Mosquitoes swarmed around the electric light. Mrs. Morgan swatted with her fan, Morgan with his newspaper. Already they had waited three years for their son to become himself again, their Jesse, the boy who had run off to Memphis, then to Chicago, then to the Pacific. This man who had returned to them from the war was a stranger, a broken man, with no center to bind his parts together.

"He needs work," Mrs. Morgan said. "Maybe he'll find some on this trip to Memphis."

They saw their son approaching, his arm around Marsha, leaning on her, his steps following hers from side to side of the lane, their voices in the moonlight mournful.

Hot winds blowing up from the delta rattled the sugarcane. Monk felt the shaking in his bones. There was a hiss as of flame among the stalks when the wind rasped through the brittle cane, like the harsh rasp of locusts that would come again with dusk. Thin spears of shadows, long morning shadows, shaken by the wind, lay in ripples on the land which had been reclaimed from the swamps near New Orleans. Monk leaned against the barbed-wire fence and watched the two draft horses standing head to tail, swatting flies. *Which way is them blessed pines.* A scrawny mare muzzled grass, then rolled onto her back and disappeared in a fog of red dust. *If old Monk could just vanish like that he'd never come back.* As the dust settled the mare solidified, her muzzle to the ground, grazing.

He knew the mailbox waited behind him—that snake arrested as it was about to strike—and he felt the power of the warden, and of the warden's huge wife, drawing him back to the house. They wouldn't remain long in that house, he knew, for he had seen seven wardens come and go. Sooner or later even the cowards and boot-lickers ran afoul of the politicians up in Jackson, and were sent packing. Now Morgan, he was a fire-eater, an ornery man, and he had just about stayed out his term at the prison. Turning away from the fence, Monk groaned. When the warden left, and the warden's wife, and little Miss Fay—dancy-footed Miss Fay—he would be left alone once more. He was afraid he wouldn't have the strength to break in a new warden. Besides, the next man might not have young ones, and an old nigger-man cast away in this place needed the young ones to keep him going.

Before scuffing back toward the brick house, he turned and stared at the sugarcane, which was waiting for him, telling him it would still be there tomorrow, still the next day, always cool as it had been cool among the pines. *You stay there because Monk don't want to be buried all alone in Skeleton Hill when there's pines waiting for him.*

By dragging his feet on the return down the lane he scuffed up a riot of dust, but it scarcely reached above his knees.

"You hear from that boy of yours, Monk?" Today it was not the warden's redheaded granddaughter who asked, it was one of the newly armed trusties, a coal-skinned man named Travis.

"Nope," the old man answered.

"If I had me a boy, and he didn't write, I'd whup him." Travis gestured with the new shotgun. The barrel gleamed from a recent oiling.

Monk glanced at it warily. "Watch where you be pointing that."

Lowering the barrel, Travis said, "Whup him with a strap, is what I'd do."

"I ain't knowing if my boy's even alive. If he is, likely he whup me."

In the kitchen Monk surrendered the mail to Mrs. Morgan. "Move on now," she scolded. But Monk only backed away as far as the doorstep, watching her leaf through the mail with her great blunt thumbs. Halfway through she stopped, tugged one envelope from the pile.

"Go on, old man," Mrs. Morgan cried, brushing the air with her hands as if shooting geese.

"Did Monk bring bad news?"

"Never you mind what you brought. Shoo!" Watching the old man hobble down the steps, she ran one stubby finger around the border of the envelope. Although her great red hands were dry and cracked from the lye soap, she wrung them one more time in her apron before carrying the letter to her husband.

"What's it say, Abe?"

"It says in two weeks we're going to be cotton farmers again." Morgan shoved the letter into a pigeonhole of his rolltop desk. "The governor says that the good people of Mississippi don't like niggers carrying guns, particularly nigger convicts, and seeing as how I won't change my ways, he's going to change wardens."

She watched his face closely to see how he felt about it all. Every night she would stand with him on the back stoop and they would read the sky for the next day's weather. Now she read his face with the same confidence, and saw that he was relieved, that he was ready to go back home.

"What are we going to do with Jesse?" she said.

"That's just what I'm trying to figure. He won't like going back to that farm, and his brothers won't ever let him forget running away."

"Maybe he turned up something in Memphis," she said.

"Maybe. We'll just have to see what we can work out."

She smoothed the apron over her belly. "And what about Monk?"

"We cain't just leave him here."

The warden swung slowly around on his swivel chair and leaned his elbows against the felt blotter on his desk. He dabbed the tip of his ink pen against the felt, watching the blue fuzzy stars form, musing.

"You could get him paroled maybe," his wife said, "and he could live at the old Wilkins place on the riverbottom."

"I'll have to have a think on that."

"Likely the next warden would lock the old man up."

The inkstains straggled across the blotter, like footprints in wet sand. The warden pondered. "Nobody would miss him if we just put him in the truck and carried him home with us. They'd think he just crawled off somewhere like an old possum and died."

From the vacancy of his eyes, and from the way he leaned over his desk, Mrs. Morgan realized that her husband wanted to be left alone, and so she lumbered back into the kitchen, scraping the horny soles of her bare feet against the floorboards as she went.

The warden opened his bank ledger book and resumed his calculations. After another hour of figuring he concluded that there was simply not enough money to set Jesse up on his own, not unless part of the old home place were sold off, maybe the walnut grove, but the warden knew his son well enough to realize that he would accept no money gained at such cost. Perhaps the boy had found work in Memphis that day. Memphis was not far, Jesse could visit the farm, perhaps he would overcome his bitterness towards his father.

Exhaling heavily the warden opened the prison register and ran his finger down the pages until he reached the first name that was not crossed through:

Monk Jones—b. 1871, Natchez, Mississippi. Father was a slave on the Reynolds Place, fought for Mississippi in the War. Monk the seventh son, twelfth child. No schooling. Occupation: lumberjack. Only child a son named Raphael by Creole woman—no address. The aforesaid convicted of second-degree murder of James Flint, mill foreman, a white man, on 26 November 1892. Jury recommends mercy on account of murder was aggravated. Sentenced to life-imprisonment. Signed this day the 27th of Nov. 1892, Paige Williams.

At the end a space had been left for recording the date of the prisoner's death, or of his "escape." Morgan carefully wrote in the date, two weeks hence, when he would load his family in the truck and leave the prison for good. *Monk old boy,* the warden thought, *we're just going to have to escape you from this place.*

Morgan then wrote a letter to the two sons whom he had left in charge of the farm, directing them to get the old Wilkins place ready down by the riverbottom, and to keep back the cotton on the hill above Moccasin Ford for seed. Then in his pocket notebook he began listing the fertilizers, the machine parts, the poisons and other supplies that he would need for the start of another cotton season the next spring. Sugarcane was not his crop. It was cotton, and he could already smell the acrid dust of the poison that would coat the leaves. As he wrote down the names and the quantities, as he began calculating the proper days for plowing, as he imagined himself walking again over that land in northern Mississippi, he realized that he would not regret leaving the prison. At sixty-two, he had found rest tempting, and so he had accepted the job as warden four years earlier. But this was not the peace he wanted—overseeing state land, raising public crops, guarding the bodies of convicts, living in a government house. He would be glad to become his own man again.

At sunset the warden was still hunched over his desk, bringing the prison records up to date, when Jesse appeared in the lane with Marsha, following her awkward footsteps from side to side of the dirt track. Jesse's cardboard suitcase dangled from his free hand, and he seemed to be talking very earnestly with his wife. He had found out something in Memphis. Morgan strained to hear their voices amid the crickets and locusts, but he could not distinguish their words, as if they spoke a foreign language on purpose to exclude him. He stood up and leaned his fists on the desk. *No,* he thought, *sit still. Jesse will come tell me.*

The voices trailed around behind the house, foreign, then they entered the kitchen, where they spoke with his wife. He would go to his mother first, Morgan thought. The voices stayed there a long time, now muttering, now squabbling, and still Morgan would not allow himself to move. Let Jesse come to him. Mrs. Morgan's voice rose and scolded and complained, but even her words seemed unclear to him. The voices of his son and his son's wife approached the front room door, passed it, and proceeded upstairs, where they sought out the granddaughter's room. Morgan could hear them asking about Fay, although what they asked he could not tell. Then he heard Monk's tired voice reply, "Miss Fay sleeping like an angel." Out of all this shouting and mumbling and whispering, that was all Morgan could decipher: the feeble words of a worn-out old nigger.

Morgan stood up and then abruptly sat down. He felt like a stranger in his own house.

Jesse's footsteps crossed and recrossed the room above Morgan's head. Twice the warden rose, to go ask his wife what the boy had found out, but his pride would not let him actually go. So he waited. He reread the newspaper. On the blotter he diagrammed a scheme for plowing down near the river. And he could not help remembering the days on the farm before Jesse had run away; before Ransome had followed and been killed trying to shag that train; before Jesse had fled to Chicago and from there, after Pearl Harbor, with the army into the Pacific; before Jesse had twisted his mind by killing so many men in those foreign jungles. You could remember, but you could not get that time back. For an instant Morgan felt desperate; there was only emptiness before him, he needed someone to talk with, anyone.

The door opened and Monk's head appeared. "Missus says, do you want your coffee in here?"

"No," the warden said, shaking his head, suddenly relieved. "None."

The footsteps continued above for perhaps two hours, and then at last they descended, paused at the door, and entered.

"Dad," Jesse said hesitantly.

Morgan swiveled on his chair. His son's face was haggard; it had not yet recovered from the war, even after three years, yet it was still his son's face, with traces of that eagerness, that rashness, that quivering of the skin, which ten years earlier had driven him north to those infernal cities. In time, Morgan could recover him.

"I'm listening," the warden said.

"You never wanted me to go to Memphis or Chicago in the first place," Jesse said, scuffing his toe on the pine flooring.

"That's a fact."

"And you blame me because Ransome tried to follow me and got killed."

Morgan did not answer. He laid his hand thoughtfully against the warm glass shade of his desk lamp.

"That's a fact," Jesse said, and as he recalled the brother's death and the funeral, the resentment he had borne against his father for ten years twisted his features. "And you never believed I could make my own way in Memphis or Chicago, free of you. And so you were glad when I didn't make it, and ended up in the army. And I bet you were secretly glad when they shipped me back here a cripple, more helpless than when I was a child, because when I was a child I still had a future."

As he spoke, his footsteps creaked back and forth over the loose floorboards. Air seeped through the cracks from the crawlspace beneath the house. Morgan waited patiently for his son to finish, and then he said:

"You never heard a word of that from me."

"But I could see it in you, I could feel it."

"Well what you felt and what I felt were maybe two different things. Anyways, all that's history."

"It's not history for *me*," Jesse said, thumping his chest one sharp blow. "It's eating me up."

Morgan stared at his son, who was trembling all over like a dog that had just been run over by a car without being killed. The son could still not stare back into his father's eyes. Damp halfmoons spread under the arm holes of his shirt, now seamed with the dust and grit he had collected during his two-day trip to Memphis for job interviews.

"Sit down, son," Morgan said. The son obeyed his father, as if by reflex. The warden moved the lamp to one side so that he could see his boy's face, gaunt and bedeviled as it was. "So what did you find out in Memphis?"

"I got a job back with that tire company. They looked at me kind of funny, but said being a veteran made up for it."

"When do you leave?"

"Tomorrow."

"To Memphis?"

"Nosir," Jesse said, avoiding his father's eyes, staring at the path of inkstains on the blotter. Weak, bewildered, he waited for his father to ask the inevitable question.

"Where?"

"North," Jesse said, in a voice almost a whisper.

"Where?"

"I'm going to one of the company's plants further . . . north . . . in Ohio." Out the window he could hear the locusts, and beyond them the faint sound—like a foreign broadcast drifting across the local radio station late at night—of the canefields.

Morgan studied his son's face, which was yellowed on the near side by the lamp, shadowed on the other. Darkness collected into pools like rainwater in that haggard face. The eyes, sunken deep in their sockets, were lowered, cutting from side to side as if hunting on the desk for something to seize upon. Morgan had to look away. The face pained him.

"That's a long way, Ohio," he said.

Jesse rose, his haunted face rising like a full moon in the yellow lamplight. "If I can get away and forget everything," he said, "I'll get well again. But I have to get away from . . . everything."

"I pray you do," Morgan said, swiveling back around to lean over his desk. "I pray you do."

Jesse stood for a moment behind his father, rubbing his hands nervously, and then he laid them briefly, lightly, like glancing leaves, upon his father's shoulders.

Morgan heard his son leave the room, heard every creak in the floorboards, but he would not turn to look. Down the hallway drifted the voice of Monk, muttering in his ancient sleep.

Next morning Monk wearied himself trying to dress Miss Fay. She wriggled out of every stitch of clothing he put on her. When he tried to hold her still she danced beyond his reach, giggling so hard that she was soon forced to plump down on the feather-tick to puff awhile.

"Miss Fay, you got the devil in you this morning!"

"Whoopee, old Monk, we're going to the homeplace!"

"Child, you never been to the homeplace. You was born here." She lacked the strength any longer to resist him, and so submitted to the starched frock.

"But Papaw told me all about it. There's rivers. And bears!" She hugged tight around his neck and roared: "There's Indians and buffaloes and windmills and everything!"

"Hold still, honey."

"Monk," she said, touching one of the bony hands as it groped among the frills for buttons, "you're going with us?"

"No, missy. No no. Monk been put here for all his days. Been put in here and forgot." The hands fumbled more than usual in their struggle to convert the frowsy toddler whom he found each morning in her crib into the prissed and petticoated lady who would greet her granddaddy with a prim kiss. She stamped her feet impatiently and squirmed out of his reach. "I'm sorry, Miss Fay. Monk's old eyes ain't too good this morning."

"I'll get Papaw to bring you with us. You've got to come along." Having decided, and having proclaimed her decision, she considered the question settled, and so scampered off for breakfast, at peace again with the world, all her buttons buttoned yet her bow untied, the loose strings billowing in her wake.

Monk watched her until the last starched frill vanished into the dining room. *Goodbye honey. Monk's gone to the pines.* Although the mail would not arrive for hours yet, he set out for the mailbox, with the dew thick on the lane, the dust too wet still to fog about his feet, the sun still lost in the glazed grass of the pasture. *Monk been put here for all his days honey.* Reaching the mailbox he paused; no more steps had been measured out to him. Then he continued on across the county road, looked once back at the warden's house, spied around for the trusties who stalked the road with their shotguns, and then he kept walking. One of the bay draft horses plodded after him across the pasture, nosing his pockets for tobacco or sugar cubes.

"None for you this morning, babe," Monk said as he patted the horse's muzzle. *Monk gone to the pines.* He smiled down at the water on his shoes, at the wet burrs sticking to his trouser cuffs, at the neat print of his feet in the damp soil, the prints he made that morning because he wanted to make them. Every step drew him closer to the canebreak. *Monk gone to the pines.* At the far side of the pasture he picked his way through another fence and there he hesitated, on the border of the canefield, at the boundary of the world he had known for over fifty years.

Inside the brake was a mass of nested shadows, an unbroken mat of darkness. The cane breathed and the sun lay still behind him, tangled in the glazed grass of the pasture. Before him stretched the cool forest of stalks, the sugarcanes that might have been pines.

Monk heard no voice, nor did he hear the wary footsteps pursuing him across the pasture, nor could he even distinguish the report of the shotgun from the burning pain that tumbled him over into the loam. He only knew that he had to rise, enter that forest of sugarcanes, cut his way through wall after wall of the closely planted stalks, because deep inside those shadows was the place he had been seeking, where he would find the passageway back to that continent of the past, and not even this terrible pain could keep him from going where he wanted to go.

"Papaw, can Monk go with us?" Fay asked. Her mother scraped grits from her chin with a spoon, but the child ignored her, concentrating all her attention on the white head at the end of the table.

"Young lady, you ain't been properly shook out this morning," Morgan said, scowling at his granddaughter in mock disapproval. "Your hair looks like last year's haystack. You ain't even tied up your ribbons."

Fay stood in her chair and pounded her fist on the table. "Papaw! No fooling. Promise you'll bring Monk with us." Marsha shushed her daughter, but the redheaded little girl would not take her eyes off her grandfather until he nodded yes.

Finally he smiled. "I guess we'll have to have somebody to rake your hair straight and tie your bows in the morning."

Fay squealed, announcing gleefully that she would tell Monk as soon as she finished her sugared peaches.

As the dishes were being cleared away, still without a word having passed between Jesse and his father, the overseer Kirkus hustled into the dining room and whispered in Morgan's ear.

The warden lurched to his feet, jostling the table. Jesse reached out as he passed, "Dad, do you need me . . ."

But Morgan shook his arm free and hobbled quickly outside onto the dew-damp grass, following the overseer. On the border of the canebreak Morgan found two trusties, Ames and Travis, hugging their shotguns. At sight of him they began shouting:

"I shot him first!"

The warden stopped short at the fence and closed his eyes.

"It was *me,* warden," Travis yelled. "I swear it."

"He's a liar," Ames said, "it was me first. Him second."

The two convicts squared off facing one another. The warden only waved his hand angrily, trying to brush it all away. Without another word he entered the canebrake. Behind him he heard their excited voices shouting, "When do I go free?" Row after row he advanced, passing through the gaps that had been made by the other man, even sometimes stepping in a print that Monk had left.

A hot wind slithered through the stalks, diminishing the shadows as the sun floated free of earth. Morgan's steps quickened, yet a voice within him cried to slow down, turn around, go home and pretend the old man had disappeared, had escaped. The damp soil clung to his boots, weighting his steps, enlarging the prints he left behind. The steps that he was following weaved from side to side, but their drift was straight toward the heart of the canebrake. The gaps in the rows grew wider, as if the old man in wading forward had flung his arms wide and beaten the stalks away from him.

Suddenly, without any change in the old man's tracks, Morgan staggered into a gully between two rows, and there Monk lay, face up, his arms hugged over his chest, his bony hands curled as if grasping, his eyes out of focus, or perhaps focused on the sky, on the furthest borders of vision.

"Monk?"

He drew the old man up into a sitting position. The body seemed to balance there, as if gathering strength.

Morgan touched his fingers to the withered throat. "You, Monk?"

After that moment of balance, the worn-out body relaxed, unbent itself, and settled to earth.

The Cry

Sometime after midnight a fierce cry woke me. It sounded like the wail of a cornered animal, screaming at death, *go away, go away.* Was it our aging neighbor, seized by nightmare? Or were the nightmare and the scream my own?

I glanced at Brenda to see if she had heard. Her leg slithered over our sweaty sheets, coming to rest between my thighs. Think no more about dying, it said. Touch me. She rolled toward me, teetering on the edge of sleep, as if one more cry, whether from my nightmare or from my neighbor's, would push her awake. In the stillness following that lone howl, she tumbled back into sleep.

Not my nightmare, I decided, not mine but the old man's next door. We knew him only by the noises he made, the furtive sort of noises that rats make when they nest in walls. Through the flimsy partition dividing our hotel room from his, we had heard every slurp of the soup he ate for supper, every grate of his toothbrush, every hark and hack in his throat. He was sick, judging by the sound of him — the palsied rattle of his spoon against a bowl, the wheeze of his breathing. Perhaps he was merely old, pettish in his movements, the way he shook the pages of his newspaper unsteadily as he read about the day's bullfights and hatchet murders. Sick or old, he was most likely harmless: the bones loosening in his flesh.

Madrid in August. We had come here, after four years of graduate study in damp England, for me to recuperate from a nearly fatal bout of pneumonia, for fresh air and sunshine; and here we lay in a rented box of a room whose single window opened beyond dingy curtains to the next cell. And through that opening we heard no surf, no birdsong, but only the mortal noises of an invalid. Our air came second-hand from him, through his window, over his soiled bed-clothes, his scumringed bowl, his hacking illness.

After that cry, no more sounds came through the wall except the gassy wheeze of his breath, like the pant of an accordion with a slit in its bellows. Hot as it was, I raised my arm to close the window, to shut off that breath, but Brenda in her sleep pressed her steamy leg against mine and held me down.

So I lay for a long time, sharing the air with him, listening to the Catholic hours pass on the bells of nearby churches.

At daybreak Brenda's knee nuzzled my groin and I awoke stif-fened with desire for a woman, any woman, and only as my eyes opened onto her waiting face, inches from my lips, did that woman become my wife.

"You're awfully friendly this morning," she said. I answered with my body.

The night's sweat oiled our skin. I licked dew from the shallows at the base of her throat, from the cove of her ankle and the hollow of her knee.

She counted the vertebrae on my back. "They're all still there."

"Shh!" I jerked my head toward the old man's room.

"Oh," said Brenda, "he's skedaddled."

"When?"

"Before you woke. He cleared his throat for a while, gargled, crunched some cereal—all very entertaining—and then he left for work."

"What do you mean, work? He sounds too sick to walk."

She gave me a sharp look. "So maybe he's going to feed the pigeons or play checkers. Who cares about him? Hmmm?"

Her hands beat back the sheet from my buttocks and drew me deeper into her, enthralling part of me while another part hobbled down those twelve flights of steps to the street with our nameless old man.

"You suppose he's all alone?" I said.

"Shut up and love," she cried, and I did.

She woke me again when she returned from the shower. Her belly and breasts were dusted with the cheap powder I had bought for her in Florence.

"If you'd stop gawking and get up," she said, "you might get some hot water. That leather-faced lady with the cardboard suitcases paid for a tankful, and there's still some left."

This was reason enough to hurry—our first hot water in Spain, the first since three weeks earlier in London. I hurried down the sagging rackety floorboards of the hall to the bathroom. It was locked, naturally, and the shower was thrumming. I waited on the yellowing linoleum, tracing the cracks with the nail of my big toe. The pattern was the same as that of the linoleum in my grandfather's kitchen, way back in Tennessee. Imagining the distance between Memphis and Madrid, I was catapulted back over twenty years into memories of reading the comics under my grandfather's table.

At last the door opened and through it stepped the leather-faced lady's daughter, who was more like doeskin. Seeing me, she clutched the bathrobe to her throat and scurried modestly away. Her calves beneath the robe glinted like wet fence-stakes.

The water was cold. It must have been pumped from some deep layer of stone, deep beyond the influence of this Spanish August. I stood in the tub beneath that glacial drizzle and understood our neighbor's tubercular cough.

Two other neighbors had opened their doors by the time I returned to the room. One very old woman hunched in an armchair, murmuring her rosary, pinching the beads with knobby arthritic hands that lay in her lap like a pair of twisted roots. She was so far from thoughts of the hotel, rocked somewhere far away in the lilt of her prayer, that I paused in the hallway to stare. With each wag of her jaw a large goiter jostled and writhed beneath her chin, as if it were a sack in which some small frantic animal had been trapped.

In another room an emaciated woman lay in bed, her head resting against a hill of pillows, the two sticks of her arms crossed on her breast. The shutters were tightly closed over her window, and in the darkness her face, caverned and white, glowed like the moon with light reflected from the television she was watching. Cartoons — I could see that much — American cartoons with dialogue in Spanish. Beside the bed gleamed the lip of a copper bowl, into which she spat once — twice — three times while I was watching.

The old man's door, next to ours, was shut. I could still hear from the night before the stuttering of his spoon against the bowl, like the last twitches of a meter before a heart fails.

Suddenly I began to shiver, with the same helpless, deathward quaking that had come over me for minutes and hours while I was in the feverish grip of pneumonia. I hurried into our room, needing to hold Brenda, to place my hands on her back where the skin stretched tight over her bones like canvas on a tent.

"What's the matter with you?" she asked. "You're shivering. Was the water cold?"

I clung to her, lips against her neck. My hand followed the tail of her blouse down inside her jeans, tugging it loose, groping for warmth.

"You sure do make it hard to get dressed," she said, fussing with her zipper.

"Hold still, love, hold still."

Hearing the dread in my voice, she let go the jeans and put her arms around me. "Oh, sweetheart," she murmured. "Please don't. Don't think about the illness or you'll get yourself all worked up again. You're *well* now; everything's mended inside." She tapped my chest.

"This place is like a waiting room for the cemetery. It's a warehouse for burnt-out cases."

"People die," she said. "They get old and they die; that's all there is to it. But you've got about fifty good years left in you — you're a spring chicken — so quit brooding."

"I can't help it."

"You *can*. Now just *stop* it," she cried, shaking me by the arms. "Don't give in to it. You are absolutely well. You've got to feel that."

"Okay, okay." I swallowed and swallowed, but the fear was stuck in my throat.

"Was it that noisy old man? Is that what set you off?"

"Him — and a woman with a goiter — and a skinny old woman who keeps spitting bits of herself into a bowl." Hugging Brenda against me, stroking her, I grew calm again.

"Don't complain, they're what holds the rates down in this dump." She forced a laugh. "We wouldn't be staying here if it weren't the cheapest hotel within walking distance of the train station."

"True."

"So, be of good cheer. Spain lies at our feet. The streets are full of sunlight and flowers and fruit." Her jaunty voice slammed the doors on all the invalids, shut my dread away in the mind's basement. She drew free of my arms, buttoning her jeans, pulling the belt tight, as if in cinching her waist she had shut off all possible thought of death.

In the streets there were flowers and sunlight and fruit, and also children and old people. Little girls sat cross-legged in the plazas bouncing rubber balls. Boys played tag around the statues, tugging at the bronze legs of horses, halting to apply licked fingers to their own scabby knees. The benches were occupied by aged men and women drowsing behind newspapers, picking nervously at buttons, staring as if sunblinded into the empty sky. The children I watched hungrily, and the old people I tried not to see.

"Shall we go to the Prado first," said Brenda, "or the bank?"

"Bank." My fingers toyed with the alien coins in my pocket. It felt like play money, yet in this country they actually bought and sold with it, and so we played along, spending it meagerly. We still had enough in the bank to last, if we were careful, until the end of September. And after September? It would be time to begin collecting paychecks, back in America, after twenty years of schooling, with my head full of words and my lungs scarred and my heart reluctant. Twenty years! What remained of all those days except this residue in my hand, this silt of memory that showed the way the river had run when the waters themselves were gone?

"Martin, watch out," Brenda called, jerking me to one side by the arm. Before I could change course I jostled the tray of a man who was selling wind-up monkeys. The toys sprawled every which way.

"Scusi," I said hastily.

"That's for Italy!" Brenda laughed. She apologized to the man in Spanish, helping him set the monkeys back on their feet.

"Cuanto es?" she asked.

"Ciento veinte." The man wound one of the monkeys, which danced spasmodically over the tray, its arms twitching up and down as it beat on a drum. She smiled at the man and his gadget, a child's toystore smile. Did I marry her for that radiance?

"Hey, let's get one," she urged. "Make it our mascot."

"I know who'll end up carrying it in his pack."

"But it's so tiny. It won't weigh anything at all."

I was reaching for my wallet, but as I watched, the dance slowed, the arm beating the drum began to falter, and suddenly all I could hear was the old man feebly tapping his spoon against the bowl. The spring winding down. "We don't really want to lug that around, do we? Come on," I said, pulling her away.

"All right," she agreed reluctantly, "but when I'm needing a monkey to dance, you'll have to dance for me."

On the sidewalk ahead of us the Spaniards stood aside quietly to let us pass. *Americanos locos.*

"The springs in those cheap jobbies don't last a week," I explained. I was afraid my tone would give me away—that creeping fear. But she seemed to put it out of her mind easily, and walked along beside me studying the shawls and pastries in shop windows. Did I marry her for that toystore smile? Or for that ability to shut each moment in its own closet, and never to open the doors again on moments that gave her pain?

"Look at that bullfight poster," she called, pointing to my left. As I looked, she pushed away from me, bolting towards the curb and calling, "Last one to the bank fixes supper!"

I watched her prance between the parked cars, her blonde hair swinging almost to her waist, and I thought of that hair as she knelt brushing it in front of the gas fire in London. Damp London, lost London. All that remained of England was her swinging hair, and this silt in my mind.

I could have drawn even with her before we reached the bank, but I held up. I preferred lagging behind where I could watch her, that quick flame darting through the crowds of dark people who gave way to her, knowing fire when they saw it.

When I caught up with her she was propped on her elbows against a marble counter in the bank's lobby, heaving for breath and laughing triumphantly. "I think I'd like beef stroganoff," she panted. "And asparagus in cheese sauce, cherries jubilee, wild rice . . ."

"Is bread, cheese, and wine close enough?"

Her laugh rang in the bank like a bell. "With you fixing, anything would taste delicious."

Maybe the diet was affecting my brain, provoking this gloom. Cheese and bread and wine and bread and cheese. Who could believe in the future after four months of margarine?

As I was handing the check to the teller, Brenda peeked over my shoulder and said, "Do not pass go. Do not collect two hundred dollars. Go directly to jail."

The teller looked up in confusion. "Perdone?"

"It's nothing," I said. "Only my wife."

Waiting for the Prado to open, we walked behind the museum to El Retiro park, which floated like a green island on the gray sea of our map. El Retiro—the retreat. And that was what I needed, what I had come to Spain for, a sanctuary where I could step outside of time. I needed to crawl out of the river that had carried me for twenty-five years, to crawl out and study the current, to walk forward along the banks to spy on my future. Was this the current I wanted to bear me, the one that flowed from school to school to windowless office, and led to the death of the flesh?

"You sit if you want," Brenda said. "I'm going for a walk."

Sunlight filtering through the leaves freckled her face as she tilted it up to me. "Don't go and fall in love with any Spaniards," I said. From my bench I watched her drift off through the woods, the butter-yellow sunlight running in stripes over her hair and down her back. My tiger. Just filling her skin, while I wore my flesh like borrowed clothes.

Motes of dust wove intricate patterns in the sunlight. Brownian motion, the physicists call it. Time, my fear called it. Each jiggle of dust canceled a second. I watched the particles dance, my life tick-ing away, the very air become a clock. The terror of death closed my eyes, and in the darkness I could hear the motes of dust softly clicking against one another. The click of the old man's teeth, the tap of his spoon, the shiver of his newspaper. I stood up, shoved my hands in my pockets, sat back down, twisted one way on the bench and then the other. *Where is Brenda? Where?*

Then I saw her off among the trees, her supple body passing in and out of sunlight, prowling.

With my head tipped back and my eyes closed, the sunlight soothed me. Warmth spread in me, coating my nerves. I imagined this was the peace a lion must feel, the day washing over his dulled senses while his mate circled closer and closer.

"What is he doing?"

Brenda's voice startled me. I opened my eyes to find her standing next to me with her arm pointing. Some distance away an old man dressed in antique soldier's uniform limped over to a bench and sat down.

"My grandfather used to call that sitting down on a bench."

She frowned at me. "No, really—just watch him for a minute."

As I looked on, the old man abruptly stood up, as if remembering an appointment, and hobbled quickly away. Then suddenly he stopped, backed up, walked around in a little circle, and headed off in another direction. In one hand he carried a cane, but although he was limping painfully he did not use it. Instead he hefted it like a rifle, occasionally fitting the hooked end against his shoulder and aiming the shaft away into the woods.

"An old freedom fighter?" she guessed.

"Probably from the civil war," I agreed. "It looks as though some of his circuits have burned out." We watched him dwindle away through the trees. As he went he continued to tack and veer and spin, as if bumping against invisible barriers, the cane lifted and ready to fire. Squeezing him out of my mind, I asked, "And what did you find on your prowl?"

"Several starving dogs, several rude businessmen—and these."

She held up three pale orchidy blue flowers that swayed on their slender stems.

"The signs say, Don't Pick."

"You and rules," she huffed. "I bring you flowers to get you out of the dumps, and you go on about Franco's blessed signs."

"Not so loud." I glanced up the path, on the lookout for soldiers or police. It seemed that every third Spaniard wore a uniform.

"I can see the headlines now: AMERICAN WOMAN LIBERATES SPANISH FLOWERS AND IS TURNED OVER TO DICTATOR BY HER HUSBAND . . ."

To appease her, I accepted the flowers, tucking them in my shirt pocket and saying, "Gift of love?"

Grinning brightly, forgiving my caution and my pettiness, she answered, "Gift of love."

Near the park gates a bulldozer was grading a slope. A crew of men with wheelbarrows, trudging back and forth along the same path like a column of ants, hauled dirt for a new flowerbed. Brenda stood gazing at them. Several of the workers gave her appreciative stares, and she stared boldly back.

I strained to catch a glimpse of the old freedom fighter, who was still bouncing along against his imaginary barriers like the helpless pellet in a pinball machine, like a mote of dust. One day soon he would recoil like a pinball from the last post, slip down through the table's hole, and disappear.

Brenda blew the admiring gardeners a kiss.

Every painting in the Prado Museum seemed to be of St. Sebastian, lashed to his post, bristling with arrows like a balding porcupine; or of Jesus hammered to his cross; or of some other tortured holy man. There were acres of martyrs, their skin torn, their wounds running scarlet, their bodies broken. Inside the paintings, spectators looked on — Marys and Magdalenes and Johns, sullen-faced, in awe of the suffering and yet not quite grasping the point of it all. Why break your body for the sake of those phantoms in your head? And the spectators inside the museum looked on as well, their faces twisting to mime the painted figures, features growing somber, puzzled, skeptical.

"What did they shoot him full of arrows for?" Brenda asked, pointing at a particularly gory St. Sebastian. "Just for believing something? And look, doesn't he seem to be enjoying it?" She shuddered.

"They were all haters of the body, those saints. Let's go find the Greeks."

In the classical sculpture gallery she ran her fingers up and down the spine of a marble Apollo, wooing the stony flesh. "Feel," she said, and placed my fingers on the stone.

The cold shocked me. I jerked my hand away. "It's like ice."

"Not the temperature, love—the *shape*."

I walked my fingers up and down the marble vertebrae, accepting the cold of this dead Greek.

Laughing, she said, "That's just what you feel like in the morning. A delicious ripple of bones, like beads for me to play with. Nice." She laid her hand softly on my back.

Before we could budge, a guard bore down on us, one great finger wagging from side to side. "Non toucho! Non toucho!"

Not touch the statues—or one another? I wondered.

Brenda curled her finger at him and raised her eyebrows meaningfully. As he leaned his ear towards her she whispered in German, "I have eaten the cat and the shoes in school today," gave him a vaudeville leer, and then led me briskly away. When I looked back from the next gallery he was still occupying the same floor tile. He had given a dapper slant to his guard's cap and a smirk had replaced his official frown.

"You brightened his day," I said.

"He must get sick of marble goddesses. A little flesh and blood would do him good." She halted suddenly in the middle of the El Greco room and stared intently at my face. Tourists bumped and elbowed against me, grumbling in a babel of languages.

"This is like a freeway," I said. "We can't stop here."

Ignoring the crowd, she said, "Your color's a lot better, it really is. In another few weeks you'll be your old self again."

Involuntarily I touched my throat. Warm. The cough completely gone. The London damp almost dried from my lungs. I would live.

"Yick!" she said, gesturing at the walls of contorted, elongated figures. "El Greco! Another body-hater! I can't take any more of this stuff. Where's the Rubens?"

Traffic was sparser in the Rubens gallery. A couple of boys scrutinized the nudes from various angles, as if hoping that from some perspective they could see behind the draperies. A frail, wispy old lady glowered up at the towering figures. Tons of flesh hung in the mammoth frames. From a cushioned seat at the center of the gallery we seemed almost to hear the grunt and moan, to smell the sweat and perfume of these straining bodies. Brenda always liked these exuberant landscapes of pink skin.

"Now *there* was a man who loved his women."

"With his paintbrush," I said.

"With more than his paintbrush! Don't tell me he could paint thighs like that if he didn't enjoy putting his hands up the servant girls' skirts." There were thighs in every direction, so I settled my gaze upon one plump pair and held my peace. "You and these mopy Spaniards can have all the martyrs," she said. "Give me Rubens! Just imagine him at ninety, modeling his latest St. Catherine on the woman who brought him his beer."

"But St. Catherine was a martyr too, stretched on a wheel."

"And she wrecked their wheels for them, didn't she? Boom! That's what fascinated old Rubens, the way her body refused to give in." We sat back to back on the tufted seat. Brenda's weight shifted softly; her breathing purred against my spine. "Now who would you rather have," she asked, "one of those scrawny insipid St. Theresas with her ribs showing, or that lusty St. Catherine right there?"

"I'd rather have you."

She gave a humming laugh, the sound of power lines in the wind.

Three gypsy women, each suckling a baby, patrolled for handouts on the sidewalk in front of the museum, their red skirts brushing pebbles over the cement, their midnight hair hugging their necks like shawls. I turned to point them out for Brenda, but she had fallen behind; she was back on the steps of the museum buying postcards from a boy whose body bent sharply at the waist, as if his lower limbs were paralyzed.

While I paused to wait for her, the gypsy women encircled me. Their dark eyes accused me. Of what? Whiteness? Maleness? No, I shook my head, no I am not the father of your children or your misery. The circle of red skirts, hem touching hem, closed upon me. Each way I turned a palm thrust out at me, dark eyes glaring. The woman who blocked my path in front held her baby up to me, and as she did so one narrow pointed dug swung out of her blouse, dry as a gourd. You have done this to me, said her bottomless eyes, you have forced this screaming brat on me, dried my milk, and now you must pay.

I raked all the coins from my pocket and handed them to her. Without a smile she turned away, all three red skirts turned away, confronting other tourists with their howling babies and their shrunken breasts. At that moment Brenda sauntered up.

"There went tonight's supper," she said.

"It was only a few pesetas."

"Did you pay for the breast, or the baby?"

There it hung in my mind, that dried tit, that withered fruit milked of its juices, the nipple a hard stem. "For the baby," I said.

"You're the original soft touch, you know that?" She gave me a scolding kiss on the nose. "Gypsies or no gypsies, we still need to go buy vittles."

We sweated our way across town toward the market. The sunlight balanced like suicides on windowledges. Brenda's hand became slick against mine, but she would not let go. Was it gypsies she feared? Or wind-up monkeys? Or some decrepit old men gaping their toothless smiles at me from doorways? Holding my hand she could tell when the terror came over me; she could sense, delicate instrument, the first tremors.

From a sidewalk vendor she bought ice cream, and as we walked along she offered me licks from the cone. The sickly watery grating ice cream of Madrid. Rotted by the heat, like the last snow man before spring.

"No thanks," I said. "How can you stand to eat that stuff?"

"It's cold, anyway."

I avoided looking at the faces of the people we passed on the street, for fear that in one of them, in the crowfeet around the eyes or the sag at the corner of a mouth, I should encounter myself. But Brenda stared at everyone.

"These Spanish women sure run to fat," she said. Her quick pink tongue curled round the melting ice cream, racing the sun. No matter what she ate—and she ate everything—her body somehow transformed it into that taut glowing flesh. "Good food and sun," the doctor told me in gray wineless London, "that's what you need to get you over this nasty business with your lungs." *This nasty business*—it was almost my last business. We could afford only one medicine, either good food in England or sun in Spain, and we chose the sun.

Wherever we walked, Brenda kept to the shade near buildings, and I kept to the light. She feared leathery skin. I feared that killing damp in my lungs. So now on our way to the market, the edge of the shadow trailed along between her feet and mine. But she had the sun inside: you could feel the radiance on her skin.

The market hall was filled with the crying and haggling of women. I watched Brenda sail boldly among them as she bought our oranges, cheese, salami and bread. Her face looked pale among the Spanish faces, and yet glowed like theirs with an inner fire.

"Hang onto this," she said.

Leaning against the apricot vendor's stall I held the string bag of cheese and oranges while Brenda picked over the plump fruits. The women glared at me as they passed. Why was I not at work? Was I a woman to shop for food? And my chalky skin, was it not sickly? Brenda was right—the young women were spindly, and then after marrying they ran quickly to fat. But between scrawny girlhood and waddling womanhood, each one passed through a moment of sensual balance, when the body invited your hands, the eyes shone, the face registered every gust of desire. That was the moment of flower, when men swarmed to the woman's scent. And in that moment, when the woman's body seemed to hold its breath, her beauty seemed permanent, and young men with hungry eyes forgot all time in their wooing. Everywhere I looked, the bodies of young women beckoned to me—the skin drawn sharp over the bones of an ankle; an elbow bent under the hoop of a basket; the saddle formed where the hip flares out from the waist. Watching them, I too slipped out of time.

Back in our hotel room, drowsy from wine and apricots, I dozed through the late afternoon.

Brenda woke me by pulling gently at my ears. "Hey," she said, "I need help."

My eyes flickered, but were discouraged by the ceiling light.

"What's the name of an English river," she persisted, "six letters long, used as a pseudonym by an English writer?" She peered at me, watching my slitted eyes for signs of life.

Words I had. My head was stuffed with them. "Orwell," I muttered.

"Of course!" She wrote the letters onto the *Tribune*'s crossword puzzle. Naked except for her bikini briefs, she sat cross-legged on the bed beside me, hunched over her newspaper, like the little girls in the plazas who sat cross-legged with skirts hitched up to their knees playing jacks.

I ran my finger along the furrow her belly made where it folded at the navel. "When is supper?"

"When you fix it."

I groaned, remembering our wager, the race to the bank. "You had a head start," I complained, brushing my fingers back and forth over the down of her belly.

"You won't get supper that way." She pinched the knuckles on my roving hands. "The margarine's in a plastic dish in the sink, and there's some ham left from lunch."

I groaned operatically and rolled over on my stomach. Soon I felt the sole of her foot shoving against my ribs, and I tumbled onto the floor.

"The oppressed male gets up and prepares the sandwiches," I said. "Scarce out of his sickbed he is forced to wait hand and foot upon his indolent wife." I began laying out the fixings for supper.

Brenda sidled up behind me to watch the preparations, her arms curled around my neck, her breasts nudging like twin questions against my shoulder blades. "Nobody who's still sick could make love the way you make love." She plucked a slice of cheese from my hand and folded it into her mouth. "Really, you're a good tight armful again. No squish under the skin, no rattle in the lungs."

"Oh, the body will pull through."

"How about the head?"

How about the head? I wondered. Will this Spanish sun bake the death out of my brain as well as the damp out of my lungs?

"Oh—" I shrugged. Against my hand the ham felt like what it was, dead meat. I stuffed it into a bun. A faint acrid taste rose in my throat. "I still have twinges now and again. Not so bad. Some little thing triggers it, and then I grope around for something to hang on to."

Brenda plopped down on the edge of the bed, chewing cheese, pondering. She drew her legs up and crossed them at the ankles, her thighs opening in unconscious invitation. "What's it feel like?"

"It's a terrible emptiness—" I waved my hands, trying to gesture at what I could not name. Margarine on my fingers, embedded in the knuckles. How could I ever eat this sandwich? Dead pig. "I see myself sinking through the dark, sinking and dwindling, like a spark falling, until I vanish. There's no *me* anymore. I wake up in the middle of the night and *know*—not like some sentence out of a book, but deep down in my blood I *know*—that my brain's eventually going to flicker and go out . . ." She watched me intently. This strange panicked animal, her husband. I would rather have strung a bead of kisses up her thigh than keep talking, but her eyes asked for explanations. "I was so close in London," I said. "I felt myself flickering—this tiny point that was me, guttering like a candle. I had to struggle just to keep a little flame alight."

"But you're *past* that now. Don't you see?"

"I know, I know, but the feeling still comes back. Some little thing sets it off."

"Like those monkeys this morning?" she asked.

"I didn't think you'd noticed."

She leaned forward, elbows on knees, chin in hands. Her breasts bobbed as she moved. "I always notice. The monkeys—and the man firing his cane in the park, the cold statue, the old people on the benches, the grunting fat women in the market. Your face doesn't hide very much. You're transparent." She cocked her head at me. My little bird. At that moment I felt she really could see into me, as if the sweat that coated my skin, like grease on paper, had made it translucent. "Like right now, for instance," tilting a siren's smile at me, "you've got something other than death on your beastly little mind."

She was right, of course. With the ham and margarine still slick on my lips, I kissed my way to her lap and lay my head there. She bent forward until her breasts fell against my face, the scent of the street and the market coming off her skin. I breathed in the day all over again, recovering lost time, pushing death away.

We loved by inches. Throughout the sultry evening, as we wrote letters and studied the maps, we touched and touched. The air became thick with our breathing; the friction of our bodies crazed the molecules.

When I lay back against the pillows, with *Don Quixote* propped open on my chest, Brenda twisted her hair into a tuft and with it dusted my neck and shoulders. The words on the page wriggled loose, escaped from their ranks, ran mad.

I kept listening for the old man, but no sounds came through the partition.

"Roll over," she said, "and I'll rub your back."

With her weight on my legs, her palms leaning into my back, her fingers massaging my spine, a glow crept through me, my mind went out, and I became my body.

"Hey," she whispered in my ear, tousling my hair. "You're like a great big puppy. You'd let me do this all night, wouldn't you? But first let's shower."

I sat up slowly, waiting for mind and body to rejoin one another.

As we rounded the corner, making our way to the bathroom, we could see the leather-faced lady's daughter approaching from the opposite direction, towel over her arm, robe kicking open at the knee. Brenda bolted down the hall and stood in front of the bathroom doorway, crying, "Primero!" The other woman turned away with a bewildered look, and hurried back down the hallway.

The door was locked. Brenda rattled the handle and thumped on the frosted glass. "What is Spanish for emergency?" she asked.

"Try 'emergenzia.' "

"Emergenzia! Emergenzia!" she cried. From the other side of the door an old woman's voice wailed in response, a feeble quavering voice which startled us both.

Through the frosted glass we could see a shadowy figure painfully stuffing its arms into a gown. A bat with broken wings. Presently the door opened and an old woman shuffled slowly out, leaning upon two canes which appeared to have grown from her knotty hands. It was the woman with the goiter. The rosary dangled at her neck, the beads glistening against her black gown, giving her an uncanny rakish air, like an old bawd in her pearls. Passing me, she twisted her face up toward mine and smiled. Toothless, the lips wrinkled, the lines of the mouth broken at the corners. And yet flaring in that smile was the echo of a young woman's passion.

I closed the bathroom door behind me and leaned against it. How would my form look through the frosted glass? My limbs sure in their movements, muscles stretched taut over the rack of bones. No bag of flesh wobbling from my chin.

"You do charm them at all ages," Brenda said as she leaned over the tub's edge, testing the water.

The tepid water drizzled down on us, the temperature of September rain. Madrid's dust washed away, and with it the day itself. Spinning beneath the nozzle to rinse her back and sides, Brenda did a slow pirouette. My naked ballerina. She leaned on my arm, balancing upon one foot while she washed the other. Then she shifted her weight, ballerina, and lifted the other foot.

"Pretty dance," I said, and she smiled, gripping my arm as she teetered on one pink foot. Our evening had been one long ballet, advances and retreats across the body, teasing on the edge of coitus. The prince chasing the queen of swans across the stage. When we hugged, her breasts squeezing against my chest formed a soft pond for the falling water.

Before the shower could run cold, we climbed out of the tub. With our lone towel I buffed the skin of her back and scalp until she begged me to stop.

"This is just like the linoleum in my grandfather's house," I said on the way down the hall to our room.

"The same cracks?"

"No, the same pattern."

"You do remember the weirdest things."

The woman with the goiter had closed her door. But the other old woman, with her fleshless arms crossed like sticks on her breast, still lay back against her hill of pillows and watched television. The flickering light from the screen passed over her face like the running shadows of clouds, projecting a vicarious life through her worn nerves.

Brenda's fingers pressed my wrist as she led me past the old man's door and into our room. Was he there yet? His terrified cry waiting for me?

"Come," she said, "off with these impediments." Her fingers crawled up the buttons of my shirt. "Forget the old ladies. Here I am."

There she was. The pale silhouette of her bikini still clung to her from the days we had spent lounging on the coast. White peaks of her breasts. Pale crescent slopes of her buttocks. My home planet. Loose hair falling, a sleek avalanche over her shoulders. Between her thighs a blond wisp and a dark valley.

"Come," she said.

She stood upon tiptoe, ballerina, and settled herself down upon me. With my hands supporting her and her fingers upon my shoulders, we swayed there for a spell, dancing slowly to the music of our blood.

Then a sudden grating sound tore into our loving—the old man's door opened, paused, slammed. Crackle of papers—a sack opening. Rough scuffle of shoes across the floor. Water running in his sink. Dull clink of metal. Cans? A gagging sound in his throat, a liquid cough, the slap of spit hitting the sink's enamel.

"Wait," I whispered. "I can't. Not while he's—"

Brenda shushed me with a kiss. She danced me towards the bed, sat me down upon its edge and sat herself upon my lap, her legs around my waist. "Just love me, *love* me," she whispered back. She drew my head against her and held it there, a palm pressed over each of my ears. The soft cushions of her breasts against my cheeks, the dust of her talc on my lips.

Though muffled, sounds of the old man still reached through the haze of love to unsettle me. The hacking cough, raking phlegm from his clogged throat. The soup poured out, breathed on. Rattle rattle of spoon stuttering against the bowl, faltering meter of his waning life.

"Me!" Brenda cried, "me, be with me. I'm here, I'm *with* you."

A hard nipple thrust into my mouth. Fists knotted in my hair. Her body rocked softly on my lap, a ship at anchor. Still I heard the rattle of the spoon and the gagging sounds from the old man's throat, but they merged with the sound of waters, with the raw tingle of skin, with the ache of our bodies that had waited so long. Brenda pushed me backwards onto the bed, firm belly against mine, my lips on her throat, my hands guiding the motion of her hips in a spiral around the thrust of my own, no sounds now, no old man ever, no walls and no clocks, no time even as we rushed and rushed over the waterfall calling and calling like gulls.

Sometime after midnight I awoke with a start. That cry again. But whose? His or mine? From the old man's room came the wheeze of breathing, the accordion with a slit in its bellows. Nightmare breathing. He was mumbling in Spanish, gurgling the words as if they bubbled up through the phlegm in his throat. He made hasty, desperate sounds, clawing the sheet, scratching the wall. Cold crept over my limbs, twisting my body from side to side on the damp bed. And then he howled—a howl for caves and midnight hilltops. I wanted to cry out in my own terror—*Don't let me grow old, don't let me die.* But I held my tongue. The chafe of loving still warmed my chest. My body denied its death. In the dark I reached for Brenda, to lay my hand on her stomach as it rose and fell, and in the dark I found her, there she was, the earth.

Prophet

. . . your old men shall dream dreams
and your young men shall see visions.
— Joel

On a sun-fired November morning, dressed in the black of doom,
he straggles like a scarecrow through the snow. About his flailing
arms the sleeves flap crazily. Beneath his boots the snow creaks.
Pounding a fist onto his dog-eared Bible, he bellows his message
down the length of Roma's main street.

"We are in the last days! The end is at hand! The Lord is coming
to burn away the iniquities of this world. He comes to judge the
quick and the dead. In a great vision I have seen the fire of the last
days!" His green eyes flash like sunlit glass and roll wildly in the
yellow dough of his face. With each snap of his jaw his beard bristles.

Folks look at him and shake their heads. Crazy old Jeremiah Lofts
is at it again. Poor soul. What his stony slave of a wife and his
ancient-seeming young sons must be suffering! Poor soul, poor soul.
In a town as small as Roma — four streets of shops vending all the
necessities and many of the frills of life, a clutter of gas stations and
pool halls and bars, a town hall and Carnegie library, three white
clapboard churches, and a hodge-podge of houses cramped like spectators at a boxing match around the town square — Jeremiah's vision
is about as unsettling as a boulder heaved into a pond.

The vision seized upon him four months ago, in the hot belly of
July. He and his five sons were building the family house, on the
side of Ledge Hill above the abandoned limestone quarry. Like his
people before him, he is a penny-scrimping dirt farmer, who must
scratch his rocky two hundred acres hard six days a week to dig a

living out of it. On Wednesday nights and Sunday mornings he was preaching to the Brotherhood of the Last Days. On other nights and the remainder of Sunday he and his sons sawed and hammered at the frame of the house, which lodged like the skeleton of some great animal half way up the slopes of limestone ledges.

No one in Roma thought he could ever get it built. But he set about the construction with that furious intensity which frightens the towns-people in everything he does — as if the energy of his black flapping figure might generate electricity like a dynamo, and discharge. He is a violent and severe man. People give him room. Like many who spend their waking hours in contact with the soil and livestock, he hates all in man that smells of animals or earth. He makes love to his wife hurriedly, without pleasure, and only because he needs sons to work the farm. She wears long gray dresses that kick at her ankles, and serves Jeremiah from a distance. The daughters may not dance or go about with boys. The sons may not laugh or carry on in their father's presence, nor smoke nor drink — nor sweat, for any other reason than work or worship.

Jeremiah has always been a deeply religious man — some would say a fanatic — but last summer, under the strain of the house-build-ing, he grew more troubled for his townspeople. He could see iniquity spreading through Roma like mold. Old man Sly added a wine counter in his General Store, which raised the number of bars to five. Soldiers sauntered down from Cleveland to dicker with the paint-faced girls. The hardware store opened on Sunday afternoons, just in case anyone was needing screws or can-openers. And then, in that dusthot belly of July, when housewives took to wearing shorts and halters into town, when boys with long hair and girls with short skirts spent half the nights roaring around Roma in their parents' cars, Jeremiah went to see the mayor, the sheriff, the five ministers, the President of the P.T.A., and the head of the Chamber of Com-merce. No one saw the evil he saw.

But for Jeremiah, these were the signs of collapse, cracks in the stone tablets of morality which his forefathers had brought with them intact to New England, from that rotten Old World. Now he smelled the stench of decay in his own town, in his nation, and in the obscure encircling world. News of wars in Asia and Africa drifted to him like the smell of rats putrefying in the walls of the barn. Many of his neighbors worked in the Roma Arsenal, the town's major industry, which was building munitions for those wars. Two states away, even such a short distance, he could hear the worms patiently working at the bodies of Negroes who had been shot and buried for trying to vote. Just up in Cleveland, not thirty miles away, there were men in laboratories culturing germs which could poison the earth.

Then, in July, when the house had been shingled and tar-papered, when the chaos of rough timbers had begun to take some definite shape, as if held together by the strength of Jeremiah's ferocious will—the decay of the world ate its way into his own family. His oldest son David was caught stealing a red-jacketed sex novel from the Globe Drugstore. When examined by the county juvenile authorities, the boy convinced them with an hour of crazed talk about scarlet whores and volcanic passions and laceration of the flesh that he would need psychiatric care. He was allowed to go home, but Jeremiah was to keep track of him, keep him away from girls, even from his own sisters, and have him report twice weekly to the clinic in the county seat.

David's sin and affliction fell upon Jeremiah with all the force of a sign from God. In a world wholly rotten, not even a man's family —perhaps not even his own soul—could be kept pure.

"It is a sign," Jeremiah told his wife that July evening when David was returned from jail, the boy's face caved in by a smile. "It is a sign from God, to alert me, to force upon me the sickness and sufferings of the world."

Sarah didn't say anything. She rarely said anything, especially to her husband, this woman whom the children of Roma called The Stone. For seventeen years she had borne his children, his pinchgut farm life, the rigor and brutality of his religion, had borne the full weight of his revulsion from life.

"He calls me away from this worldly existence, into His service. So I must go up and seek a word from Him." Jeremiah's bottle-green eyes grew hard again, glinting like bits of fire, the way they always turned when he felt inspired. "This very night I shall go up onto the hill and seek Him out."

Sarah listened in silence over her sewing. There were the patches to put on bluejeans. The boys hated being teased for wearing the patches, but there was no helping it. They scuffed through the knees so quickly, with their rough-housing. Tonight as on every other night she submitted in silence to his Biblical tirades, as she submitted to the impersonal ferocity of his body when for the sake of children he allowed himself to make love to her — yielded to all the fierce needs in him. And so while he consulted with God, she sat in her rocker, sewing the tough denim patches in the circle of lamplight.

The July night was clear, with stars shouting and limestone bursting from the hill like cold froth as he climbed to the top ledge. Jeremiah stooped down for a drink at the moss-lined fissure where chalky water poured from a spring. Even in the middle of summer the water swelling out of the rock was ice-cold, yet winter never could freeze it. He thought of Moses in the wilderness, conjuring water out of the rock with his staff. Next to this spring, Jeremiah fell on his knees to pray. Above him the stars snapped, remote and frozen. Behind him the water gushed from the stone. About him hung the pungent smell of ferns and damp moss. His mind was all a silent waiting.

He prayed for David, his son who was lost. He thought of when the boy had come home, accompanied by sheriff and doctor, with the broken smile twisting his face, and he heard again the boy's words: *It was their eyes, father, their eyes and how they stared at me, the women in the picture — They stared at me and asked me something I couldn't answer, couldn't even understand, but it was me they wanted it was me — And do not worry, father, it is dying, my body, I am killing it.*

Jeremiah could not weep for his son, but he prayed fiercely for him. And beyond David he prayed for his town, his nation, for the whole world, with its billions of rats stinking in lost corners.

At the thought of the vast suffering and sin on earth — at the thought, like a snapshot, of his own soul perched atop this limestone hill and locked in speech with Almighty God — Jeremiah grew violently excited. For he suddenly realized that he — *he* — was the chosen man, the last messenger between heaven and earth. Suddenly he knew that the Lord was calling him to bear the final words to the world. Yes, he knew it, in his bones he knew it, and yes, *yes!*

he answered. He ached with the glory of it. From so low to so high! Out of a man who had scratched at the land for a scant living while struggling to lead his family and his own soul in the ways of right-eousness — out of such a man the Lord had chosen to make a prophet!

For a long while on that ledge he sweltered in the fire and thunder of his discovery. He was a prophet. And he was to utter the Lord's judgment upon all the earth. And the Bible said it would be by fire next time. And so it would be — the end of the world in flames. Wrapped up in the frenzy of his revelation, Jeremiah again heard the words of his son: *Is it a sin father a sin to touch the slick skin of the books and to look the women in their eyes? Is it a sin my father this flesh I wear my body O please please make it no sin.* And then Jeremiah knew — his son David, born the 30th of June, was the sign. His next birthday would be the world's last day, when the fire would roar through all the earth.

Jeremiah shuddered. He did not think it, did not feel it, but sud-denly he knew it, knew it in the branchings of his nerves, when the world would end. In that instant of vision he put off all the guilty weight of the sin-ridden world.

As he strode down the hill, still in a daze, his will seized upon this knowledge. Back inside the tar-papered husk of a house, he found his family asleep. Instead of crawling into bed next to Sarah, he wrapped himself in a woolen Army blanket and lay outside under the creaking elm, above the quarry where he had often gone as a boy to pray. His will was tempered by the fire of his vision. And he lay awake for hours on the limestone, beneath the wheeling stars, and beat out the plans for his future mission over the rigid template of his will.

Far below in the Mahoning Valley he sensed the dark surge of the river. Over a period of centuries, the river had eaten into the tus-socked banks and so changed the path of its dark body on the way to the Ohio River and thence to the sea. Here was movement and growth beyond human lifetimes, like the revolution of the heavens, like the hidden shifts in the guts of Ledge Hill, like the spring which never failed: the subtle, glacial movements of the hand of God. The stars, the rock, the river — Jeremiah lay all night under the creaking elm and felt at one with them all, as the agent of the Lord's mysterious workings in the world.

In the morning he did not shave, and forbade his sons to shave. The family ate breakfast in silence. Their father had been possessed again and there was nothing to do but wait until the spirit burst forth. Sarah watched her husband warily. David would not look up from his bowl. He knew the other children would blame him for driving their father away again into his world of demons. So David winced when Jeremiah began to speak: "The Lord has granted me a vision of the times to come, and fearsome times they will be. The sin and affliction of our son David has been a sign unto me."

David dragged the queer twisted smile onto his face, that imbecilic grin he used to cover every muddled feeling. Then suddenly he leapt from the table and ran without a word from the house.

Jeremiah did not seem to notice. Sarah and the children ate on in silence, waiting for the demon to leap from him, as if by shouting the devil into words he might kill it, and become again their father. They watched the struggle in his face—the demon this morning must be ferocious. Around the green glassy eyes and the taut lips, his yellow skin jerked into grimace after grimace. It was a misery for Sarah and the children to watch him twitch with the effort of chewing his demon into words.

"On the ledges, at the mouth of his everlasting spring, the Lord granted me a vision," Jeremiah continued. Sarah watched him closely. Overnight he had aged. He had not come in to sleep beside her. And, in her modest way, last night after the trouble with David she had wanted to have her husband's body next to hers. Not for passion—she had learned she was not to feel passion—but for the weight and firmness of him at her side. Again he gathered himself to speak:

"It was the last judgment and the passing away of this world. God revealed both time and event. It shall be almost a year hence, on the 30th of June—for the evil of our son David, and of David's birth, is the sign. And the end shall be by fire."

Even the older children were still frightened by these thunderous outbursts from their father. They squirmed in their chairs and struggled to keep their eyes away from the demon twisting his face. His voice seemed to them weirder than ever before, as if it came from some echoing cave and not from their father.

"And the Lord has chosen me to prophesy in this town, so that a remnant might be saved. I must warn those who will hear me. We shall leave off the building of this house, for earthly mansions will not protect us. We shall not touch each other, for we must put aside things of the flesh for things of the spirit."

Then Sarah knew why he had taken the blanket in the night and gone outside. She knew, and she felt shrivel in her womb the hope of a last child, a child to make up for the misery of David, felt it die as if the foetus had already been conceived in her womb and had perished.

And so, as Jeremiah shouts his prophecies in the Main Street of Roma on this sunfired November morning, he has left Sarah untouched and fallow in what she is sure will prove to be the last fertile months of her life. And so the beards of the older boys grow modestly, like dark silk, fine and thin like the silks of corn, and their hair crawls down over their ears. Jeremiah's own beard sprouts like black wire from the yellow clay of his face. The tar-papered house remains half-finished, as if it were the abandoned shell of some monstrous snail. Snow humps over the warped stacks of lumber, which have been paid for by years of scrimping and worry, and which, like Sarah, now lie untouched. In the yard, snow makes delicate frozen fountains out of weeds that in the fall went quietly to flower and quietly to seed. For these four months he has prepared himself for his prophetic mission. And now he carries his message into winter-drowsy Roma.

Folks have always said he was crazy. But this is something outlandish even for Jeremiah Lofts—to stand all in doom-black clothes, ankle-deep in snow, and bellow ferociously down the length of Main Street about the end of the world by fire. Roma is too small to ignore him.

"We are in the last days! The Lord comes to burn away the iniquities of this world! Come before Him and repent, for the end is near! I have seen it in a great vision, the fire of the last days, and the time is not far off!" Roaring, he flails his arms for emphasis, in the snow-buried street just outside Mario's barbershop. The windows fairly rattle. The handful of Saturday-morning men and boys (some there for haircuts, most for jawing, or listening to the farm report) scuttle to the door and stare out at this bellowing prodigy.

"Jeremiah's gone off the deep end this time," says Don Himes. Veins burst in sprays of red beneath the parchment skin of his face.

"What's that cracked old bastard up to now?" Fred Wayne asks. Studying brassiere ads in back copies of *Life* while Mario shaves him, Wayne is the only man besides the barber who does not rush to the door.

"Hellfire and damnation and the end of the world," Himes answers.

"Is that all?"

"Tell him if it hasn't started burning yet, he can come in here and warm himself," Mario says.

Himes waves out at the prophet. "Hey, Jeremiah, come in and thaw yourself. Mario says he's not ready to meet his Maker . . ."

On great wooden strides through the snow, Jeremiah approaches the candy-striped barber-pole. Like crows dispersing at sight of a rifle, men and boys scatter from the doorway to chrome-armed chairs at the scrape of Jeremiah's boots on the steps. Snow slips off his hat and boots, droplets slither through the fine black wires of his beard. His stare runs over the faces of the other men like a hand. And then he shudders into speech: "I have come to warn you to put aside your evil ways and return again to the Lord. Repent, for the end is near."

"End of your infernal preaching, or what?" Wayne calls from beneath his lather in the barberchair.

"Not my end only, but the end of every man in this room, the end of Roma and everything beyond Roma—"

"Front end or back end?"

"Sounds like ass end to me," Mario observes, his razor skinning lather from Wayne's jaw.

Jeremiah hushes, looks slowly from face to jeering face. Under the queer cracked fire of his eyes the smiles quickly melt again. There is something frightening in his intensity—something darts at them from his eyes, sparks at them from the filaments of his beard. In the moment's silence his words seep through the coarse gravel of their age, down into the deep caverns of their religious childhoods, into the almost-forgotten memories of days spent in Sunday school, nights spent at Bible readings. And down in those depths of nearly forgotten beliefs, Jeremiah's words stir visions of hellfire and sword-wielding angels, black sheep and white, trumpet calls and terrible demons on horseback, visions of flaming furnaces and earth-swallowing floods. Visions they thought had been safely drowned beneath the years since childhood. And now this man — this Bible-thumping, black-hatted scarecrow of a madman who calls himself a prophet — this man has come to rouse these visions. No face smiles.

Jeremiah knows this: that in each of these men there hides a latent prophet, back in the visionary caverns of childhood. But unlike them, he has never abandoned that past, has never allowed the gravel of age to bury his earliest beliefs. Memories of his own father roaring out passages from the prophets and Revelations, memories of his uncles and grandfathers seething with the spirit around wood-fires in the Lofts' parlor, of women leaping up during prayer meetings among the Brotherhood of the Last Days, possessed and wild-eyed — these impressions are as fresh for him as yesterday.

"Thank you for the warning," Mario says. "We don't mean to poke fun at you —"

But the prophet, after that hard stare around the jeering faces, marches out. As he crosses the street the men laugh again — but nervously.

And so things continue. For a moment Jeremiah's words disturb the placid waters of Roma, stir up strange fish in the depths — forgotten fears, forgotten beliefs — but soon the surface calms. Still, he goes about preaching — in the grocery stores, in Sly's bar, at the Shell gas station, on the playground of the elementary school, on the steps of the Free Will Baptist Church, beneath the war memorial in the town square, around the movie theater where spindly boys and ripening girls kiss with the sound of crickets in the shadows. His smoldering green eyes, his wire beard, his fist and his dog-eared Bible become familiar to the townspeople, yet they remain as unsettling as snakes.

His reputation rides like a monkey on the back of Sarah as she hurries silently around the stores. Some of the women whisper that she has turned the old man mad: the wife of any man who sees so much evil in the world must be a little wicked herself. At school the small girls with their pigtails bound in rubber bands, and the older girls with hair piled on their heads like grass, all avoid David, and gossip about his sisters in the lavatory. The boys have passed it around, about David's stealing the book, and all the queer things everybody claims he told the psychiatrist. The schoolchildren agree that they always could tell he was "off," on account of his creepy grin, his dangling skinny arms, and his stink.

The winter passes and then the spring, with Jeremiah's ghost wrapped about his wife as she skulks through town, and about his children as they suffer through school. Hot weather comes, but Jeremiah's clothes do not change: coat and mud-flecked trousers, boots and flat-brimmed hat – all as black as doom. David and his brothers and sisters flee school into summer vacation. For Sarah, however, there is no release.

As June begins, Jeremiah's preaching becomes even more frantic. His mission rides him, rides him, until he grows gaunt under the furious weight of it. This last month in this last summer, his clothes hang loosely on him, as if the demon that rides his soul also consumes his flesh. His sallow flesh sags like muslin over his skull, hollowing his cheeks. These hot June nights Sarah hears him rise from the mat he has spread for himself on the bedroom floor, hears him get up and pace the hall, mumbling broken prayers. Several times he climbs again to the top of Ledge Hill, but receives no further visions. Sarah lies very still and listens, hoping that in the dark he will come and touch her. Perhaps in the frenzy and agony of his soul he will walk quietly through the dark and touch her. But no.

Now: a week before David's birthday, the last week of Jeremiah's world. The prophet's voice pitches higher and faster, like a speeded-up phonograph record. His arms wave more violently. Out of their sunken sockets his eyes burn more disturbingly. From his wagging jaw his beard bristles more fiercely. Some of the children are frightened by his jerky motions and inhuman bellowing. Their parents are less frightened by what they see in him than by what they cannot see, by the unknown fiend that has seized upon his body. They can no longer predict what he will do or say. His mission — or his madness — has ridden him into some demonic region where the minds of Roma cannot follow. Increasingly, when he corners them in stores or on the street, they are scared by the uncanny ferocity of his prophecies — ferocity alien to this Ohio town, whose buildings creep up to the square like distant relatives at a funeral.

For half a year the townspeople have suffered Jeremiah's ravings, partly for the humor of it, partly from fear. For a spell he was a curiosity — like Miller's new harvester, or the two-headed calf, or the spring carnival held in the Methodist churchyard. But now he becomes a nuisance — or worse: for some people his frenzied message of damnation has actually grown terrifying, not because they believe him, but because they simply don't *know* any more. He seems so convinced.

So during these last seven days of June, with corn cracking the dry fields, Jeremiah's violent doomsaying drives the citizens to desperation. Finally a posse of mothers confronts the mayor, claiming that Jeremiah has attacked little Sharon Lyons. Attacked her? Well, they say, at least he scared her, and in running away she fell and ripped open her knee. Other children cannot sleep, and lie awake nights moaning. Besides, this prophet is giving the Roma Arsenal a bad name by standing at the gate and bellowing about peace and love. The man is a danger to their children and their livelihood. He needs to be put away. And so the mayor calls the sheriff, who arrests Jeremiah beside the granite war memorial in the square.

Sheriff Leeland stops at the cell and looks through the bars at the man in threadbare black who stands with arms upstretched like a scarecrow at the iron-barred window. "You want me to tell Sarah you're here, so she can bring you by some of your things?"

"Yes, yes, if you would," Jeremiah says in a quiet voice he has scarcely used for twelve months. It is dry, brittle.

The sheriff's heels click away over the tile floor of the jail. Jeremiah listens wearily — almost relieved, in his exhaustion, that the stone walls keep him from preaching any longer. *Friday,* he thinks, *and tomorrow Saturday and that is the end O my Lord.* Out the window, which is level with the sidewalk, legs and dogs amble past. Beneath boots and shoes and the bare feet of children, dust puffs into tiny clouds. As the evening stretches out, trousered and naked legs scissor their way toward the cinema, and in two hours sidle back by again, each set of four legs hesitating and hurrying together as if holding up some single animal.

At the cumbrous metal sounds of the door, he turns. Sarah enters with a sack of clothing, a towel, food. "The sheriff says you will be here until Monday, Jeremiah . . ."

"We shall none of us be here on Monday," he answers firmly.

Children and overwork have aged her, especially during the past year—she can feel it like a heavy coat on her back. David has been a strain, the poor child's mind so confused, and there has been Jeremiah's work on the farm to make up. She hesitates. "But until—for as long as you are here, you must dress decent. Perhaps the doctor will come to see you tomorrow."

"I need no doctor."

"No, of course not," she agrees mildly, in the voice of a woman who covers with a quilt of simple words any emotion which is not religious. To his back she speaks again: "And won't they let you come home, for tonight at least, if—if you will stop—"

He turns upon her fiercely: "I cannot put off the burden God has placed upon me! I cannot be silent while I have the breath to speak." Again he turns away, stands at the barred window with his black arms lifted to the wall on either side. Several of the passing feet halt, transfixed by his shouting, then shuffle on. "Keep the children near you," he says more softly, "and have them pray. They must be ready, Sarah. After all this suffering, at least they must be ready. And David—David haunts me. Pray especially for David."

Sarah stands meekly just inside the door, like a guest, watching him. Suddenly he whirls around and pins her with his eyes: "*You* believe me, don't you?"

For a moment she does not answer. It has been so long since she has probed into her own beliefs that there is a great inertia to overcome. She thinks of the house half-finished, of the children bedeviled through school, of David sin-ridden ever deeper into strange rooms of his mind, of the child-seeds dried up within her. For eighteen years she has nursed him through his visions. His demons have been her demons. All the life she has remaining, she has through him. And she knows that, whatever he believes, she must believe in him.

In a quiet voice she says it: "Yes, Jeremiah. Yes, of course."

He catches himself on the verge of a smile, tenderness nearly betraying him. "Then go and prepare the children, and prepare yourself."

She lifts one hand, timidly, to touch his shoulder or the back of his turned head, but flinches away, and without another word departs.

Through the entire June night he prays. For almost a year he has pleaded with the souls of other men. Now he must turn in upon his own. There is so much of his life to recall, so much to explain to God, that terrible figure of lava with eyes of lightning and voice of thunder, that giver of visions and worker of miracles. Can he make himself ready in time?

After an age of remembering, the morning comes. The thirtieth of June — David's birthday — is a day of heat, no rain, no clouds, just blistering sun. Life in Roma travels the ordinary ruts of Saturday. Here and there, behind closed doors, a mother tells her children that the crazy man has been shut away. Late-sleeping men leave their whiskers unshaved. Boys stain their baseball uniforms on grass. Stores open and deal out their wares. Still, here and there, on a few faces, a quiet soberness flickers. Everyone has heard the date and the prophecy so many times that the event has taken on a frail, insane reality in their imaginations. Neighbors greet each other with "Happy Doomsday!" Jeremiah's months of prophesying have finally worn this faint impression into their minds.

As the day stretches toward noon, with the sun standing on end in the streets, dust collecting in the corners of the windows, sidewalks emptying for lunch, Jeremiah kneels at his cot and prays. Afternoon sifts into evening. Neon signs glow with colored life on Main Street. Bars fill with rowdy Saturday night crowds. Pairs kissing and squeezing each other sway in a tide toward the high school, where a band hurls music into the night. Time twists like a worm through Jeremiah's brain, slowly, almost imperceptibly. He waits for the end. The thirtieth of June drains away in fragments of sun and dust and dry starlight.

For hours, Jeremiah watches the placid evening sky. Where is the final storm? At last, just two hours before midnight, clouds arrive swiftly on high winds and blanket the stars. Far off, in the last shred of this last day, the thunder he has been expecting speaks to him again of the God whose secret he has borne like a blasted embryo for almost a year. Like a pregnant woman, he has been infused with a weight of life he cannot understand, whose growth he cannot control or deny. Like a pregnant woman, he has nurtured with the flesh of his own body a vision of the future. Now, after a year of gestation, this terrible birth is upon him.

Thunder and sudden ragged fangs of lightning rip at the tissue of the night sky. In the expanding fury of the lightning, in the violence of the thunder, Jeremiah feels the force of God, senses the ferocity of his own vision. In the leaping, flaring, jagged shots of lightning, in the volcanic, shattering shouts of thunder, he feels his life-work coming to fruition.

And suddenly he is frightened. Everything will be annihilated! Even corn sprouting in the fields and mothers tying the shoelaces of children, even moths and wood anemones and the smell of manure. Everything! The enormity of the loss overwhelms him. Until this moment the final fire has lurked in God's future, an abstraction, but now it surges up before him in all its roaring, searing, obliterating horror. All humankind, all the fields, all that is born and grows, will be scorched away. After a year he suddenly thinks of Sarah. He lets himself think even of her body, young once next to his own. And outlined against the eruptions of the night he sees his five sons, growing into straight rods of young men, and sees especially David with the pathetic grin and pleading eyes. He wants suddenly, passionately, to let the world go and return to his wife, go back to the good work of scraping the earth for food and building the house alongside his sons, go back to Ledge Hill and sit on the limestone to feel the permanence of the earth beneath him, and to watch at night the certain wheeling of the stars.

Overpowered by these yearnings, with the storm lashing ever more violently toward midnight, Jeremiah collapses from the window onto his knees and prays feverishly that the Lord in this last glint of time might spare the world. He begs that the earth and its people might be spared the judgment and the fire. With all the passion of his soul, he hunches upon the cold tile floor and pleads, wrestling with his God. Around the neck of his one-year prophecy he clamps his will and squeezes.

The clocks do not halt. Roosters report as usual on Sunday morning. The citizens of Roma lift their heads from pillows, yawning, and in some of those tousled heads a nagging question lingers. The worriers look out their windows for reassurance, to make certain that things are still grinding along in the same old rut. They never truly doubted that Jeremiah Lofts was crazy, of course, or that his prophecies were foolish. But still, it is a comfort to plant one's feet on the cool wood of a bedroom floor and to see the sun crack the horizon.

Jeremiah lies numb and chilled in his cell, worn out from wrestling with God. Nothing in his life has ever been so terrible as that wrestling, not all the years and months and days of persecution added together were as awful as that single hour in the grip of God. And now for reward, instead of rising this day with all the saints into glory, he must return into the earthly streets and fields and go face his jeering neighbors. Let them jeer, let them believe their own virtue has saved them. Jeremiah knows the truth.

He gets up stiffly from the jail floor, strips away the sweaty black suit and puts on the clean shirt and overalls that Sarah brought for him the day before. He thinks of her, of David and the other boys, of the farm and the house waiting for his hands, and he begins calculating what he will need in the way of lumber and nails, fertilizer and seed. With eyes closed he stands at the barred window and lets the early sunlight bathe him. Gradually, as the warmth penetrates, he stops shivering. On a telephone pole just outside the window a mockingbird sits, reeling through its repertoire of songs. Jeremiah does not regret any of this, not the sun nor the bird nor even the sound of automobiles cruising past filled with hypocrites and blasphemers on their way to church. He has preserved every speck of it from annihilation. But he knows it is not preserved forever. God will deliver new warnings, set new deadlines, and come storming forth again and again for that awful wrestling.

The Fire Woman

Reed Bradley stumbled home drunk again, fell asleep smoking on the couch, and set the shack afire. Mrs. Bradley sniffed the smoke as she was ironing a neighbor's wash in the kitchen. Swiftly she woke the six children, wrapped them in blankets, towels, rags, in whatever came to hand, and bundled them into the night fields. By the time she had gathered them into a shivering clump next to the privy, flames licked through the eaves and smoke thickened over the roof.

Tired, her arms and back still aching from the iron, she stood with her children and watched the fire feast. There would be no stopping it now, not till every scrap of wood, shingle, and tar paper had been devoured. Twice before, Bradley had set the old couch smoldering, but each time she had doused the stuffing before it flamed. This time, however, the place was lost. Fire had claimed it.

And Bradley had not come out. She watched the door, waiting. Would he escape? She recalled the sight of his bloated body sprawled on the couch, the spittle gathering around his slack mouth as he snored. I can still go get him, she thought. The children huddled about her clutching their rags and blankets, whining, "Where's Daddy? Where *is* he, Mommy?"

"Shush," she scolded. "He must be out driving his truck. I haven't laid eyes on him." She watched the door. *Should I go in there and fetch the pig?* The answer convulsed her: *No I hope to God the bastard burns after all the hell he's put us through. He's brought the fire on himself, the drunken pig, and he can damn well die in it, for all the years of pain, pinching pennies, and begging and scrap-ing to make do.*

Flames ate into the frame of the house. The tar-paper walls flared like tinder. The shingles crackled, smoke billowed from every open-ing, from door and window and charred walls. The intense heat forced her to shoo the children back away, toward the woods and the spring-plowed fields. That's done it for the bastard, she thought. But just as she turned, no longer even wishing his death, long past fearing he would wake and walk out, he staggered coughing and swearing through the doorway.

"There's Dad!" the children squealed. "Dad's been in the fire!"

Mrs. Bradley felt suddenly exhausted; all the day's work weighed on her. She hated the man stumbling toward her with a ferocity that wrenched her body. Not all the years of drinking, beatings, pinch-penny shame, not even savagery against the children had ever made her hate him as much as she did at this moment, seeing him emerge alive from the burning shack.

She waited with her children near the edge of the field, bracing herself, her face glared with fire, her back cooled by the dark furrows. Bradley slouched toward her, his fat-bellied figure stark against the orange flames. While he coughed smoke from his lungs and pawed at his eyes, he turned to watch the skeleton of studs and rafters disintegrate. Every few seconds sparks pitched straight up into the night as a timber collapsed.

There was little for the fire to eat, just the family's scant posses-sions, and the flimsy shack itself, two small rooms of scrap lumber. Bradley made no move to save anything. He stood gasping, stupidly watching his house burn. Although she knew there was precious little to save, Mrs. Bradley thought it just like the man (whose eyes, still glazed with whiskey, flared with the orange of the dying house) that he dared nothing. Grogginess swelled his face with stupidity. She looked away in disgust, a little frightened by the intensity of hate she felt for him.

The children hovered uncertainly about him like tiny moons, their hands seeking him, as if reaching for something secure in this dizzy night. Yet they would not actually touch him. Their eyes spread wide and their mouths sagged open as they peered from the fire to their parents and back again to the fire, bewildered by everything. The baby whimpered.

"Shut up your bawling!" Bradley shouted, then turned on his wife. "Shut the brat's mouth." Without answering she snuggled the infant to her breast, and soon it hushed. "I could have burnt up in there," Bradley screamed, waving one fist at the fire. "You *wanted* me burnt!"

"And a good riddance," she muttered.

"Just you go on," he warned, and shook the fist at her.

"And nobody'd have missed you, for all the good you ever did any of us, you drunken fool—"

He struck her on the mouth. She staggered backwards, then tumbled, with the child clutched across her breast, onto the yielding loam of the field.

"You *should* have burned!" she yelled after him, as he fled toward the county road where his diesel rig was parked.

She felt the children tugging at her fallen body, clinging to her, the baby rooting and whimpering at her breast. Small urgent hands felt her bruised face, patted her thighs in the dark, seeking some flesh that was steady and warm in this strange, strange night.

On the road Bradley's truck whined from gear to gear, hustling away. Well, she thought, he's running again. Nothing but embers remained of the shanty. For eleven years she had kept that house for him, had borne him child after child, without ever knowing the man inside the body. Now, in less than half an hour, the shack and man were gone. Strange that all should vanish so quickly. A few sparks flicked up into the darkness. Charred boards lay like blackened bones on the earth. The metal frame of the couch glowed faintly. Nothing else stood upright, except the ironing board where she had been finishing the Martins' laundry when she first smelled smoke. *O my God,* she thought, *all Mrs. Martin's sheets and pillow cases burnt to a cinder.*

With that thought pestering her she herded the children together and headed for the Darrows' barn, which hulked on the far side of the plowed field. The Darrows had grudged so little before, surely they wouldn't grudge the use of their barn. Following her, the children glanced back over their shoulders at the last flickerings of their home, dizzied by all that had happened so swiftly. They straggled over the furrows, bumping into each other, a covey of quail scurrying about the hen, scrabbling for the position nearest their mother. Every few steps the small ones had to run to catch up. One fell down crying, exhausted and bewildered, so Mrs. Bradley curled him under an arm, the baby still clutched like a sack of potatoes under the other, and she continued on toward the barn. There, atop the feedsacks, among bales of hay, the seven of them huddled together and slept. No child even made a trip to the weeds for a piss. None would dare it, dare leave this large, warm body which lay like a powerful animal in the midst of them all that long and terrifying night.

Before dawn she woke and lay still, waiting for one of the children to stir. For a time she tried to guess which child slept where, what knees and shoulders pressed against her in that nest of hay. She did not even think of the house. That was gone now, burned. Nothing in the place mattered anyway—except Mrs. Martin's laundry. No, nothing bothered her about the fire except that Bradley had staggered out of it alive. She was too hardened to care about the bruises, the shouts. All she remembered was that puffy, drunken body stumbling from the furnace she had hoped would kill him. And now, she thought, I'm already beholden to Mr. Darrow for his barn and no telling who else next.

The first stirrings came with the first light. As soon as one scrawny body stretched, all six began wriggling. The children were used to sleeping together in one pile, for each night their mother would lay them all sideways on the pallet, ranked from smallest to largest, and each morning she would find them snarled together into a heap.

So sleeping together was not strange for them. What was mysterious was the smell of hay, the touch of their mother's radiant body among them, and the spectacle of sunlight filtering through the cobwebs that laced the barn's windows. In the daylight they quickly forgot what seemed like bad dreams from the night before. Soon they were scampering around the barn, poking heads into the oats barrel, calling to the cows, throwing fistfuls of hay, daring one another to go look at the bull that stamped and snorted in a stall by himself. Meanwhile the baby lay still beside his mother, as if not quite reassured by the sunlight, not quite free from the night's frightening dreams.

"You!" she cried, in the hard voice which she knew the children would obey. "Stop that — get out of that — come here and quit poking your noses into everything." Already she could hear Mr. Darrow clanking milk pails in the cooling shed; soon he would be coming to milk the cows, and she wanted nothing out of place. The children crept back toward her and sat still while she raked fingers through hair gone awry, brushed loose hay from shoulders and bottoms, jerked pajamas into place, buttoned buttons, smudged away dirt with her licked fingers.

Before she could smooth and dust her own smock, however, Nathan Darrow sauntered whistling through the barn door, a pail dangling from each hand. He stopped short at the sight of these raggedy kids and this fierce neighbor woman in his barn so soon after dawn. He broke off his whistling and set down his pails in confusion. "Good morning to you," he said, trying not to look directly at the woman in her nightdress.

"Morning, Mr. Darrow," she answered. "We're just leaving."

"And what gets all of you up this way so early?"

"The house burnt up."

She said it with so little expression in her bruised face that he stared at her more nakedly than he ever had before, waiting for some feeling to show. "You mean you had a *fire* last night?"

"I fear so."

"And you slept here?"

"Yessir."

He looked from the nested hay, which he imagined still warm with her sleep, to the woman herself. "Why in Lord's name didn't you come by the house?"

"We didn't want to put you out. And we didn't think you'd grudge the barn. Now we thank you," she added, drawing the children about her, "and we'll just be going."

"Going where?" He stared unashamedly at this woman whose steady, dangerous eyes refused to flinch or ask for help, even with her face battered and her house burned down and her six children hungry.

"Somewhere," she answered.

"Now listen, you take the kids up by the kitchen and Rebeccah will give them some breakfast. Go on, now, it's no trouble." And she obeyed. He watched them go, the strapping woman, shapely in her nightdress, surrounded by the ragtag of children. Darrow could not go see the house until he had milked the cows, which already lowed complaint at the weight of their full udders.

Breakfast over, the seven Bradleys plus the Darrows, plus other neighbors attracted by the smoke, plus the usual array of dogs, meandered across the freshly plowed fields, past the privy which seemed forlorn in the daylight, to the smoldering ashes of the shack.

"Not much left," Darrow said.

"Not much," Mrs. Bradley agreed. She pushed one toe into the ashes, not very curious, not really caring. There were a few metal things — cutlery, a handful of twisted toys, the skeleton of the couch. The mail-order catalogue, whose charred pages remained intact like layers of silver leaf bearing the ghostly images of unpurchasable merchandise, turned to dust on her fingers. Smoke seeped from half-devoured timbers. Besides that — nothing, no warmth, no flame.

The neighbor kids rooted excitedly among the ashes, amazed at this overnight wonder, then ran off to spread the news. But the Bradley children kept deathly silent. The older ones helped their mother search, groping in the ashes for bits of metal or glass which the fire had left behind. The younger ones stood back, terrified by this sudden gap in their lives. Night, the time they feared most — for it was so often filled with angry shouts, the crash of furniture, heavy thuds and their mother's crying — had stolen their house. They watched her figure stooping in the ashes, to learn what it all meant.

Soon the smallest two began to cry. The older ones who helped their mother search kept studying her face to see what they should feel, to see if it was all right to cry; but she kept her blackened jaw tightly closed, and so they held their own tears.

"Let Rebeccah take the children back to the house," Darrow offered. "She can get them some clothes and we'll think what to do next."

"We don't want to impose . . ." Mrs. Bradley began, always wary of favors, reluctant to accept what she could not repay.

"It's no bother," Darrow insisted. So the children walked back with Mrs. Darrow — all except the baby, whom Mrs. Bradley kept with her, balanced absent-mindedly on one hip. After a few minutes, giving up her search in the ruins, she walked away from the shack and stamped the ashes from her feet. She stood holding the child unthinking in one arm, as if not feeling his weight, not even hearing his sobs, and stared at the charred earth.

"Whatever are we going to do now?" Darrow wondered aloud. He still had his sleeves rolled up from the milking, and the hair of his forearms glistened with water. The cows were served, but he would be late for work at the arsenal.

"I surely don't know," Mrs. Bradley answered.

"Where's Reed?"

She didn't care. All she remembered was that he had walked out of that burning house alive. Yet she couldn't tell this neighbor that her husband had deserted her after setting the house on fire in his drunkenness and beating her in front of the children. "He's hauling a load of steel," she lied, "a truckload out of Youngstown."

"This will likely upset him."

"Yes, I reckon it will." And she thought — I wish to God it had killed him.

During the morning practically every neighbor who lived within half an hour of the Bradley place came to survey the remains. Not that there was very much to see — just the charred earth with its coating of ashes where the shack had stood, the yard littered with misshapen utensils and trinkets which the fire had blackened but not consumed, the weathered privy with its crescent moon carved in the door. What fascinated them most was the woman, Mrs. Bradley, gray from head to foot, her dress the crude gray stuff she always wore, her hair peppered gray prematurely, her skin smudged the gray of all the ashes she had sifted and breathed since the night before. A hefty child rode easily at her waist, his legs straddling one of her hips. She was a big-boned woman, built for hard work on the land. A very parable of mute suffering, the women said. But the men said otherwise. To them her calm had the treacherous look of thin ice; a person could crack through that placid surface and drown. The fish, they said, swam deep in her. Although she looked gray to them that morning, it was the gray of river — powerful, relentless. She would outwear any man, they said. And they were afraid of her.

"Morning, Mrs. Bradley" — "Morning Ma'am" — "It's a shame, a real sorry shame, Mrs. Bradley —" One after another they greeted her, these neighbors whom she knew mostly as a servant, as the woman who washed and ironed their clothes. In the front yard the warped sign still stood, thronged by weeds but untouched by the fire, proclaiming as it had for nine years — WASHING AND IRONING DONE HERE — ASK INSIDE. Her reputation for hard scrubbing and punctual service was so high that she always had more offers of work than she would accept. With the birth of each child, however, she had taken in more laundry and more ironing. Only once, when the fourth child drowned in the creek, did she actually reduce her load of work.

Thus she was cut off even from these good people who had come to see the fire's leavings and to offer their help — cut off because she had served them, had depended on them for pay and small favors over the years, gifts of hand-me-down clothing for the children, baskets of food at Christmas and Easter, rides to town and rides to church, a thousand tiny kindnesses she knew she never could return. Only with their help had she scrimped enough to keep her children in decent clothes and passable health. And every charity left another layer of sediment on her soul; after each gift she re-treated further inside that shell.

Little enough help had ever come from her husband. More than all the weary hours of scrubbing and ironing, more than the shame of his drinking, more than her own narrow days, she, who had been reared to take pride in making her own way, resented this depend-ence on neighbors. Wherever she imagined Bradley to be — off guz-zling his last dollar in booze or sleeping in some stinking whore-house — she damned him. No, she owed these neighbors too many things to ever feel comfortable around them.

"Morning, Mrs. Bradley. I know this all must be quite a shock to you. It's a terrible thing, terrible." It was Cyrus Miller, the minister, comforting her with the pastoral tone he used for funerals and for his cows. Like Darrow he was a part-time dairy farmer, and had rushed to the Bradley place as soon as he had finished with the milking. Not in his familiar black Sunday suit, but in overalls and blue sweat-stained shirt, he looked strange to her. "We'll have to find you and the children some shelter until we figure out what else to do. Amy will see about some clothes and some beds. I'll just discuss this matter with some of the other folks."

While his wife parceled out the Bradleys among three farms, Miller spoke to the men and women who still hung around the site of the fire. A township meeting was arranged for the next evening in the village hall.

Chairs scraped on the floor of the village hall, which was still littered with sawdust from a square dance, as Miller rose to open the meeting. Dressed now in his Sunday clothes, standing rigid next to the lectern that bore a wooden eagle, he began in his earnest sermon voice: "We're here, as most of you know, to decide how we're going to put Mrs. Bradley and her kids back on their feet —" And so the talk continued, the voices of farmers and mechanics and munitions workers, addressed to a hall full of familiar faces. Everyone agreed that the community would have to build the Bradleys a house. Although they haggled over the kind of house, no one challenged the idea of a house itself, for the issue was clear: this woman and these children were their own people, and must be provided for. Within an hour the men and women agreed that every family in the township should be asked to contribute towards the materials, and every able man should volunteer two Saturdays a month for the actual building. Joe Martin, who was the county's finest barn-builder, would oversee the construction. Nathan Darrow would order the lumber and blocks through the Roma Arsenal, where he worked, for he was always the shrewdest about managing such things. Cyrus Miller would be entrusted with the funds.

No one even mentioned Reed Bradley. Everyone in the hall knew him to be a drunkard who beat his wife and shunned church. Twice while Mrs. Bradley was pregnant he had deserted the family for months at a time. Some even suspected him of drowning that child in the creek. (He claimed that he had tripped and dropped the baby while walking out one night to shush its crying; before he could think what to do, he said, the baby was drowned like a dog; and Mrs.

Bradley, who had never left the house, said, "Yes, I reckon that must be how it happened.") No one expected him to care for the family now. The mother and children were the community's care.

When Darrow told Mrs. Bradley what had been decided at the meeting, she looked away and said, "Thank you kindly, that's good and generous of you all." She didn't know which was worse—living in other people's homes and eating their food, or having the township build this new house for her and her children. In either case she could never repay, she knew that, as surely as she knew the smell of her own body. Yet they had decided to do it, so she said thank you and waited patiently for them to finish their work.

"Mom, the Bradley kids talk like hill people," the Darrow boy said in a rush as he entered the kitchen.

"Shush," scolded his mother.

His eyes followed her gaze and found Mrs. Bradley seated at the kitchen table, where she was silently cutting the tips from green beans.

"You go play," Mrs. Darrow said. After he had departed, she stacked canning jars in a kettle of boiling water. "Children talk," she apologized.

But Mrs. Bradley knew it was not just child's talk. She had heard others speak of her kind as squatters, intruders who brought nothing with them into this corner of Ohio but mouths and empty hands. Yes, she was an intruder here. Her mammy and daddy had starved in the worked-out coal fields of West Virginia, where she and Reed had lingered two years after marriage, with no work and little bread. But still she would not feel ashamed of where she came from, nor would she tarry a week in these parts if there were any work back home.

"Have you been to see how they're doing on the house?" Mrs. Darrow asked.

The other woman mechanically aligned the string beans, sliced off their tips, pushed them across the cutting board, then reached for another handful.

"I said, have you been to see the house today?"

"No," Mrs. Bradley finally answered.

"Oh," said Mrs. Darrow, stymied by the woman.

No, she had not been to see the construction today, because every board they added added to her debt. No, she had not been to gawk and look grateful as they seemed to expect of her. She did not enjoy keeping track of the debt they were building. She would have to move in there soon enough, inhabit her debt, dwell within the walls of their charity.

"Why, you've cut your finger," Mrs. Darrow said in an astonished voice.

Mrs. Bradley looked down—and, yes, she had.

"Let me get some cotton." Mrs. Darrow hastened from the room.

Yes, there was blood running onto the cutting board, and it was her blood, but it did not matter, there was more of it, there was enough to keep her alive and beholden for many years. Move the green beans a safe distance over the table, then let it flow, let it flow, let the weakness come, let the dizziness swarm in her mind and abolish her debt, only let there remain strength enough for the children.

By summer's end, scarcely four months after the fire, the house was finished. In September Mrs. Bradley and the children moved in. Although the privy still stood out back—a stark box of weather-gray wood—the new house had a toilet inside. The walls now were of concrete block, the floors were no longer earthen but wooden. While the men had worked steadily at the construction, the women of the township had gathered linens and kitchen utensils and a supply of food, just to give the family a start; by the time the Bradleys moved in, therefore, the house had been well provisioned.

The children already knew every nook and cranny of the place, for they had haunted the building site all the hot summer, had watched every stage of construction from foundation to attic. Mrs. Bradley had sometimes watched the building also, but from a distance, usually with the baby squirming under one arm or playing in the dirt nearby. She felt responsible for all this effort, all this expense. Every brick laid and every joist hung weighed on her, for she had no part in the buying or the building. During the months she and her children had spent in the various farm houses, she had worked and worked until her bones ached, but still felt that she had not earned her keep. It had always been her way to undertake any work her body could do, believing that sheer strength of body would keep her free of debt. But now she realized with despair that no amount of work could repay the gift of the house. As the humiliating debt increased, her hate grew for the man who had caused it all and had survived the fire to run away.

Bradley had never appeared during the building. The men joked bitterly about him as they worked through the hot months. For Bradley himself they did not give a damn, but, "That woman and those kids he's gone off and left," they would say, "they've got to be provided for." Often that summer, some man who rested for a moment in his work looked at the raw-boned woman standing in the distance, sinewy arms crossed over her breast, powerful and sturdy as stone, and thought she would have made some man with guts a hardworking wife, if an awesome one. "She'll wear out ten Reed Bradleys," they liked to say.

To the children the new home was no less mysterious for being so familiar. Instead of the one pallet they now had two; now they went to sleep every night in two neat rows and woke every morning in two jumbled piles. Using the toilet indoors was strange and called for endless experiments. The neglected privy became jail, outpost, hideout, den, as game gave way to imaginary game. Everything in the new house smelled queer, everything felt and even tasted queer. And it was glorious fun to be all together again, the one wild pack of them, without their father's lurking violence to terrify them in the nights.

Meanwhile, during those early days in the new house, their mother made the place her own by shifting every stick of furniture at least once, touching and rearranging every can and every thread of linen. When the house was settled she replaced the old signboard in the yard. Again it was announced to one and all: WASHING AND IRONING DONE HERE — ASK INSIDE. Neighbors again brought her their laundry, for they knew she would need the money. Still no one had seen anything of Bradley.

After days of hesitating, Mrs. Bradley finally asked Darrow if he would write a letter to the people of the township, a letter to be tacked up on the village hall, thanking everyone for this work of charity. Although she knew that the people of the township gave ungrudgingly, she still felt in their debt. All her life—first in the house of her coal-mining father and then in the house of her truck-driving husband—she had struggled against the *need* for other people's charity—the company's charity or the state's or the township's. Never had she been able to stand absolutely free. Now her husband had dragged her lower, and the children with her.

Months passed without word from Bradley. Mrs. Bradley managed the house on the money earned from washing and ironing. Her hands were chafed raw by the lye soap, her arms ached at night from the wringing and ironing. Yet she did not mind the work. Having the house clear of that man was all she asked.

Then one night he came back. Without knocking, he barged in the front door. "Cozy little place we got here," he said.

Mrs. Bradley dropped the iron on the board. "There's no place for *you*. Get out." She would not shout because the children slept in the next room. "Get out, you."

"Is that any way to treat your old man?"

From the first gurgling sound of his voice, the first disgusting lurch of his body into the room, she wanted to lunge at him.

"You're no husband of mine," she answered. "Now you just get out of this house. We don't want you, we don't need you." Her hands lay clenched against the front of her skirt; not a muscle moved in her bony face.

"I'm here and I'm staying. It's my damn house if it's anybody's."

"You kept away just long enough to let them get it finished. You left us to sleep in the field."

"I knew people would look after you."

"You didn't care a damn."

"Look, all I want is a night's sleep. You're my wife, you bitch. A man's got a right to his woman . . ."

"Don't you touch me."

"Come here, come here and shut up."

"No!" All thought of the children sleeping dissolved in the flood of pent-up hate. With a revulsion so powerful that it shook her entire body, she yelled at him, "Get out! Scum! Pig! Riffraff! You leave us crawling to the neighbors, then you come strutting back like some dog, thinking I'm another one of your sluts—"

One hand slapped hard against her jaw and she reeled backwards. "Worthless drunk!" she screamed, and spat in his face.

Then he grabbed for her, dragged her rolling onto the floor, clumsy in his drunkenness, kneeling on her stomach and pummeling her face with palm and fist. All the time she kept screaming at him, clawing at his chest, while he shouted, "Shut up! Shut up, you bitch!"

Screaming, kicking, slashing at him, she squirmed from under him, struggled to stand, but fell again as he tugged her down by the dress, upsetting the ironing board in her fall. The iron struck his shin, and as he grabbed for the pained leg she balled her fists in his hair and rapped his head one furious blow on the floor, and then another, softer blow.

She rolled away, panting, sobbing, and stared at the body of her husband, now limp, unnaturally still, that body swollen by years of whiskey. The face was more bloated, the bags under his eyes deeper, the clothes shabbier and hair thinner, but it was the same man she had hoped would die in the fire. Now as she lifted the iron and watched his motionless skull, even as she flexed her arm to smash that hated face with its slack features, she suddenly lost all desire to hurt him. Had he died in the fire, she would never have seen his corpse; had he stayed away, she could have forgotten him. But now that he lay at her feet, still and vulnerable, blood seeping from the scratches on his face, hair matted with sweat, the inert mass of his body twisted by anger and pain—now that she was confronted by the man himself in all his weakness, she could not bring herself to kill him. The arm hung slack at her side, and the iron tumbled onto the floor.

Only then did she notice the children. They were huddled together near the bedroom door, completely mute, listening to their mother whimper, watching the blood trickle over the head of this fat body which lay sprawled at her feet, a man whose face only the three oldest even recognized, and which only the very oldest could be sure, absolutely sure, was his father's. For many moments they remained in that shocked silence, eyes staring as wide as their small faces would allow. Then the younger ones began to whimper in sympathy with their mother. Before she recovered from her daze, the children were clutching at her legs and waist, and, like her, they were blindly and helplessly crying.

When Darrow answered the knock at his door that evening he was surprised to see Mrs. Bradley, surrounded by the small covey of children, again dressed in odd blankets, towels, and rags as they had been on the morning after the fire. "Well, hello, Mrs. Bradley. Is anything the matter?"

"I fear so," she said.

As she stood there expectantly, not moving, not offering to say anything, only staring at him in her dumb way, yet obviously very troubled, Darrow went on: "Something wrong with your new house?"

"The house is just fine, Mr. Darrow."

The children, like their mother, stared at him as if expecting some sort of explanation.

"What *is* the matter?" he said.

"We need you to call a doctor. Bradley came home tonight and he's hurt."

"Hurt? What happened?"

"We had a fight," she said, her words coming in a passionate rush that startled Darrow, "we had a fight, and he got blooded up pretty bad and now I can't get him to wake up. I didn't mean to hurt him so bad, but I'm not going to put up with nothing more off him."

Only then did he notice the cuts and bruises on her face. It seemed all bone, her face, all bone covered with skin as tough as leather. Yet even that tough skin could not mask the trembling at the corners of her mouth and eyes. "You just be kind enough to call the doctor for us," she said, recovering her usual grave manner, "and we'll be on about our way."

"But what are you going to do about Reed? You're not just going to walk back in there?"

"Never you mind. I'll tend to my own husband."

Refusing all invitations to come into Darrow's house, she gathered her children and turned back towards her new home, that safe and warm home, those walls of debt, which had been the gift of the community. Watching the clump of them straggle in the moonlight over the stubbled field, Darrow thought again how much they looked like a covey of quail, the chicks swarming about the mother hen. The children scrambled, hustled, and bobbed across the uneven ground. But the woman marched straight over the harvested field toward her home, where her husband might still lie motionless on the floor, or where he might simply be waiting.

Time and Again

I awake from feverish sleep to the thunder of jets overhead, which reminds me that I must go this morning for x-rays at the airbase. The daylight world knifes into me. I realize that I have dreamed all night of being captured, put on trial, and executed by robot officials whose armies I have refused to serve. Dream speech lies with a sour taste on my tongue. Awareness of the slaughter in Africa rises in my stomach like nausea.

Struggling against my fear I roll over to find that Sharon already lies awake, watching me, her chestnut eyes slick with tears.

"Hello, world," I whisper. But she will not smile. The worry on her face has become so habitual in recent days that it seems molded into her skin.

"Gordon," she says, "I couldn't stand it if you went to prison."

"I'm not going to prison," I answer, throwing the covers off and beginning to dress. What else can I do but bluff, since I feel caught up in this governmental machine which is driving me to war or to jail? For days now I have felt helplessly in its grip, like a bale of meat on a conveyor belt.

"You're lying to me."

"What do you want me to say? I'm not a prophet." I wrench a shirt from its hanger, huddle over the simmering radiator. In the pipes I hear trapped water gurgling through a valve, as if into freedom, only to be pumped round again through the system. I feel like the water, trapped in this quarrel with Sharon, trickling through the same phrases we have used so many times before.

"But if the x-rays show your foot is healed," she says, "they'll draft you." I tug at my jeans, lace my boots, wrestling against the words that are beating their way into me. "Won't they?" she insists.

"They may just lose track of me."

"They never lose anybody."

"Maybe they'll decide I'm not worth the trouble of prosecuting."

"If you're against the war, they prosecute."

"Maybe I should get into graft or rackets. Or industrial espionage. Or bribery. Them they don't touch."

"Gordon, for Christ's sake, be serious."

Every word we say I sense ahead of time, as if we are rehearsing a script. The prevision chills me, but I cannot resist. "Maybe they'll declare me politically suspect."

"They've drafted outright revolutionaries. They won't balk at a two-bit conspirator like you."

I comb my beard, parcel keys and coins and wallet among my pockets, fetch my gloves. Lying on her side, head propped on one bent arm, she follows me about the bedroom with those tearslick eyes.

"You're forgetting to limp," she says.

"Limping won't fool anybody."

"You promised! Oh," she cries in frustration, "you're not even trying. You're going like a sheep to the slaughter."

"Sharon, Sharon," I whisper, limping my way to the bed.

She draws away from my hand. "You're going to slink into that hospital, aren't you, and they're going to say you're ready for war. And you're going to say you won't go, and turn yourself in, and go to prison. And for what? Who's going to give a damn? Except me."

"Maybe the war will end," I say as I bend down to kiss her, trying to keep the anger from my voice. But it is already *in* my voice, I can hear it rising like water in the radiator.

"They'll start another."

"The orthopedist may say my foot's no good for the army. Won't hold up. Cost them a fortune."

"You know you're fit."

She is right, which maddens me. I kiss her on the forehead,

between those gleaming eyes. For the first morning since a rockslide crushed my left ankle, nine hobbling months ago, my foot signals no pain. I imagine the nylon joint shifting silently in my ankle as I walk around the bedroom. Every time I think of that plastic inside me, knowing it will outlast my flesh, outlast even my bones in the grave, I feel a twinge of death.

"You're not limping."

"Would you rather have me crippled?" I snap.

"I'd rather have you outside of prison."

"Well you just keep at me, and I'll want to go inside." I slam the bedroom door behind me.

Going down the stairs I am frightened, because the chill of pre-vision grips me again. I can see the next few seconds of my life laid out before me as if in time-lapse photography: my stumble at the foot of the stairs, my touching the knobbed post of the banister, my answering the phone. In fact I pick up the cold instrument before it rings, and through the earpiece I hear the voice I expected, saying the words I expected.

"Gordon," says my sister, "if it's a matter of money — if you think the doctor would fix his report for a fee — I can make that right."

"You don't understand," I answer, hearing my patient words a fraction of a second before I utter them, "I don't want to buy my way out of the war, or trick my way. I'll win by force of argument —"

"Or you'll go to jail like a sap."

"Or I'll go to jail."

Even her peevish sigh I recognize before it creeps through the wire into my ear. "You sound like such a zombie. Is this you — or a tape recording? You're stumbling into this like —" And while she searches for the word, I already hear it approaching: *like a sleepwalker,* and she says, "—like a sleepwalker."

"Goodbye, sister," I answer numbly, wanting to say more. But the earpiece feels leaden in my hand as I lower it to the cradle of the telephone. Even though I want to say words that will secure her to me with the hooks of love, I *see* myself hanging up, and that is what I must do.

Like a sleepwalker I make my way into the kitchen, where the same water seeps through another radiator. As I scramble eggs and stir grits for breakfast, the chilling prevision leaves me, and I am free to think. Once again I feel at home in my body. The smell of eggs is new when it reaches my nose, the frayed terrycloth napkin new to my fingers. Every second comes to me fresh again, like a gift.

Riding the bus as far as Roma, the snowskinned countryside sliding by me in stark shades of black and white, I can think of nothing except those two hypnotic moments of prevision. I have experienced *déjà vu* before, but never twice in one morning, and never for so many seconds at a stretch. Each time the spell of awareness comes over me suddenly, as if a switch has been thrown in my mind, and I *know* everything that will happen to me, every sense impression, every gesture by people around me, until the switch is thrown again and I am tumbled into my ordinary consciousness. Psychologists describe it as an illusion. But none of their explanations persuades me. I don't believe these are moments from some previous lifetime either, don't believe in reincarnation or ancestral memory, in prophecy or reversible time. I don't believe this foreknowledge comes from dreams or simple coincidence. So I am left with the experience itself, which I can name but not explain. *Déjà vu.* Foreknowledge. Prevision. It comes on me like a seizure, and just as swiftly withdraws when it is done with me.

When the bus enters Roma, crunching between the heaps of plowed snow, I realize that I have gone a stretch of two hours without thinking of the war. At least my seizures, whatever their cause, have eased me of this constant fret.

At the moment my boot touches the salted parking lot of the bus station, the switch is thrown again in my mind and I am possessed by foreknowledge of the next second, and the next, and the next. As I walk through the snow toward the highway where I will try to hitch a ride, I feel split in two: one version of myself marching ahead, a fraction of a second farther into time, and a second version walking behind, filling the footprints left by the first. I shake my head, trying to clear the illusion away. But even this gesture I see a moment before I make it.

Standing at the roadside with my thumb hanging out in the direction of the Roma Arsenal, where I must go for my x-ray, I sense each car a moment before it tops the rise approaching me, sense even its make and color. After stamping numb feet in the snowdrift for twenty minutes, I know that the next vehicle to appear—a van, reeking of paint—will stop for me. And it does. I hear what the driver will say to me even before he leans across to open the passenger door. "Damn fool day to be going anyplace, with or without a car."

I know it is a question, and so I say, "Roma Arsenal."

"It's where I'm going. Get in."

Paint fumes from the rear of the van wrap round my throat like a scarf. The man turns to me a face already familiar, right down to the broken eyetooth and under each eye the slash of bruised skin. "What business you got at the arsenal?"

I tell him in detail about the crushed foot, the synthetic ankle, and today's x-ray which will decide whether I'm fit material for the army. Between sentences I want to shush myself but cannot, because I hear the future words already leaking out of me.

"Korea," he says, tugging up one pantleg, and beneath it the leg of insulated underwear, to reveal a shin with a long scar the bleached white of dead fish. "Steel pin in there. Hurts like the devil in this weather."

Helpless to resist the pressure of whatever is driving me through time, I say, "Korea was the first of the stupid wars." I wait for him to lift his wounded leg onto the brake, to say, *Get the hell out.*

Instead he gives a brutal laugh and says, "I tell myself that every time it gets cold and this leg starts kicking up."

The switch has been thrown. I am delivered back into real time again. I am left to wonder about each new second as it comes to me.

For the next twelve miles, until we reach the chain-link fence of the arsenal, we talk about the war in Africa, about his people and mine, about where I played high school basketball and where he did, about truck stops, about pigs. All the talk comes fresh to me. I open each new minute with excitement, as if it were a package. Then as we cruise between the World War II tanks which guard the entrance to the arsenal, the driver says, "Rustbuckets. If I could just get the contract for painting all them old crates in olive drab, I'd be a rich man."

Suddenly the switch is thrown again, and I am trapped in that divided awareness—half of me dwelling in the present, half projected a moment farther into the future. Like a sleepwalker I hand the guard my papers at the gate. Part of me clings to my paranoia, fearing I will be suspected of some crime, that my name will appear on the list which the guard skims with his thumb; but part of me *knows* he will wave me through the gate. The knowledge is so much stronger than the fear that I do not give in to the paranoia. I stamp my boots on the doormat, waiting for the future to hustle me along its fixed rails.

When the guard looks up I flinch inwardly from the words he is about to say. "Physical, eh?" handing me the paper. "Looks like the big green machine finally caught up with you, buddy."

I pile in next to the painter again, fumes of turpentine gripping me by the throat. The guard waves us through the gate: and I remember water seeping through the radiator valves, circling forever through that closed system. Somewhere on the edges of my mind I feel the faint pressure of understanding, but I cannot tug the idea into the center of consciousness, because the center is filled with my awareness of the next moment.

"Hurt much?" the painter asks, nodding at my foot.

"Not any more."

"That all's kept you out of the war?"

"That—and conscience."

He snorts. "Conscience don't cut no butter—" and I can hear the guard's words playing back through this man with the bruised eye-sockets; "no butter at all—with the big green machine."

"It's not as good as a mangled foot."

"What'd they say about your conscience?"

"More or less what you just did." I imitate his snort, and his laugh rattles through the van.

Black insulated steampipes, carried on steel posts, snake along beside the road, then cross over our heads as we near the hospital. They spread in every direction, like smears of black crayon drawn against the snow. Inside them I sense the glistening steam, hustling from boiler to warehouse to machine shop and eventually back to boiler.

"What are you painting?" I ask the man.

"Fences."

"This place is all fences."

"Damn near. Ones I'm painting is where the commanding officer's daughter keeps her pet deer."

"Deer," I repeat, imagining the dappled creature pacing the circuit of its fence.

"Here's the boneshop," the painter tells me. The windowless hospital hulks in front of us, humpbacked like a gymnasium.

"Thanks for the lift."

"You bet." Just before the van door slides shut, the painter turns his bruised eyes on me and says, "Keep out of the war if you can."

I nod, feeling real time leak again into my mind. When I approach the hospital, I am free, or at least I imagine myself to be free, not knowing from moment to moment what I *must* do. This is what frightens me about the prevision; it eliminates all illusion of choice; when I am in its grip, the next word, the next action is dictated by some force outside myself. Because I do not know when the switch will be thrown again, I think furiously about how to resist whatever power is taking over my mind.

I know ahead of time the chocolate-colored face, the eyes with their inflamed lids, which the x-ray technician will lift towards me. "What unit are you in?" she asks.

"I'm not in any. I'm a civilian."

"Oh. I was wondering who'd let you wear that beard."

Against my will I feel my hand lifting toward my chin, feel it pinch a tuft of whiskers. My confused smile feels as if it is being drawn on my skin from outside. I am a blank: emotions are scribbled on my face, tape-recorded words speak through my lips, invisible wires jerk my limbs from pose to pose.

"Just relax, and hold quite still," she says, positioning my foot over the photographic plate. Sitting on the table, frozen in the position she has given to me, I sense the energy shunting inside the x-ray apparatus. In a few seconds I hear the hiss of electromagnetic waves slicing through my ankle. Then silence. I do not know whether the switch has been thrown again, or whether the power which is manipulating me has simply paused. So I sit, limp on the starched skin of the table, like a puppet with my strings slack.

A bell sounds, and my strings are jerked taut again. The technician brings the developed x-ray photographs to me in her milk-chocolate hands, which I want to grasp but cannot. I want to hold someone, anyone, want to drag myself out of this puppetshow.

Spreading the photo against a viewlight, she studies the white outline of my nylon ankle. "Any pain?"

"No," I hear myself answer.

"Neat job. A really neat piece of work."

Staring at this ghostly skeleton of my foot, I think, *that is not me. They have slipped this synthetic flesh into my body, but it is not me. They have danced me to this hospital and propped me on this table, but they have not invaded my true self. I am hiding from them back here in the catacombs, where their instruments will never detect me.*

"Take these with you to the doctor," the technician says. Still I cannot force my fingers to touch her, as I accept the x-rays.

Despite the tang of peppermint on the doctor's sterilized breath, I can still smell in my clothes the turpentine from the painter's van. The doctor's hands are cold as they rotate my foot, testing the ankle. "Does that hurt?"

"No."

"How about that?"

I shake my head. Or rather—my head is shaken. I have lost all sense of acting on my own desires. I feel myself *being lived.*

"No problem there at all," the doctor says. "A very elegant piece of surgery. Who performed the operation?"

I cannot answer. I am mesmerized by the spectacle of myself sitting on the examination table, my naked left foot jutting over the edge, the doctor's sterile hands manipulating my body. *This is a film, I am watching myself in a film. That is why it has to happen this way. That is why I know every word a second before it emerges, every frame a second before it snaps into focus. I am merely mouthing the lines of a film I have seen before. Seen how many times before?*

In a fit of terror I slither from the table, groping for my sock and boot. The doctor does not notice my fear as he scribbles a note in the folder where he has placed my x-rays. ". . . Full radial extension . . ." he is mumbling to himself as he writes, ". . . functional normality . . . recommend primary service category . . ." Now he faces me, but does not look into my eyes.

"You could be in the infantry with that foot. March all day. Front lines." He jabs his pencil in the direction of my foot, now buried in its boot. "That's all," waving a sterilized hand toward the door.

I watch myself trail through the labyrinth of the hospital to the exit. On the curb, my back turned against the hunchbacked boneshop, I stamp feet that already sense numbness creeping into them from the snow. Overhead in the darkness I hear the hiss of steam hustling through pipes, losing its heat to the outside air. At the gate the guard looks up from his magazine, squints for a moment at my face, then waves me through.

Near the antique army tanks, their treads encrusted with snow, I wait for my first ride. Headlights pick me out of the obscurity for a moment, then let me go. My thumb grows stiff from flagging cars that I know will not halt. Finally the Buick arrives which has to stop for me — and it does. I know beforehand the squirrel tail that dangles from its antenna. Before the driver opens her mouth, I hear her first sentence. And I know before I open my own what I must answer. But we have our conversation anyway, hurtling down the tunnel of our headlights, because the film will not stop.

On the bus I am granted a few minutes of freedom. These moments of lucidity are coming further and further apart; the spells of foreknowledge are lasting longer each time. Through the window I watch the snowcovered landscape gliding past in the moonlight, all the earth a shattering whiteness and all the trees and houses black. This is some alien planet, I tell myself, where all colors are reduced to shades of gray, a planet silent and bleak and cold under a cold star. Suddenly the focus of my eyes changes and I am staring at my own reflection in the bus window. Because of the dim light I can only see empty sockets where the eyes should be. My mouth appears like a dark slash in my beard. Through this reflected skull of my face I glimpse the night country seething by, and I am frightened. I want to smash the window. But I know there is no escape out there.

At the last stop before my own, an enormous woman boards the bus. As she eases her way down the aisle toward me, her black coat flapping against the seats, her bag of groceries lurching right and left with the motion of her body, I feel the weight of foreknowledge pressing on me again. It squeezes my brain with an actual physical pressure, as if the woman pressing her way up the aisle were a piston, shoving the future before her. When she asks if the seat beside me is free I want to say *no,* but I nod my head *yes* because I am forced to, and for the same reason I accept the bag of groceries that she hands me. There is no room, she explains, between her own lap and the seat in front of us. And you, such a thin boy, you have so much room, you won't mind helping an old woman like me.

Even her groans and puffs are familiar, as she adjusts her bulk to the seat. Thrusting my nose over the edge of the bag, I know what I will smell: cinnamon and garlic. When she speaks to me I smell the same flavors, and love the old woman, even though she seems to have brought my prescience onto the bus with her.

"No night to be alone on a bus," she says.

"I'm gong home," I explain.

"To a mother?"

"A wife."

"You should crawl into her arms, and stay there."

To my own amazement, I am crying. Hoping she won't see, I turn my face away to blink at that other ghostly face in the window, and it waits for me there, the empty sockets opening like hatches onto the nightcountry outside. The hope is pointless, because I know what she will say next.

"My husband never let himself cry. Never once, that I knew of." She fishes a plastic-coated snapshot from her purse, and holds it near my eyes. "He was a soldier." I glimpse a tiny man engulfed in gold braid, visors, gloves. "You're not a soldier, are you?" I shake my head. "I knew you weren't when I saw your beard. That's why I wanted to sit with you — to find out how you've escaped."

"I haven't — yet," I answer.

"You won't," she says matter-of-factly, as if predicting weather. "Nobody does. One way or another, they get you." Once again at the edges of my mind I feel the slight ache of understanding. But I cannot locate the spot. The moment passes. I am hustled on through time, already hearing her next words. "This war is awful. Where is it now? I can't keep track." Before I can answer she continues. "There was a war going before I was born, and there's been one more or less all the time since then. Took every man I ever cared about, either for a while or for keeps."

I want to answer the hurt I hear in her voice, but I am not allowed. All I can do is gather my gloves and knit cap in preparation for my stop. She senses that I am going, and says, "Here, take a pomegranate."

"No thanks. Really."

But she is already drawing the slick red fruit from her grocery bag, and handing it to me. "It's full of vitamin C. I don't eat them myself. I only buy them out of habit."

"For my health, then," I say, accepting the pomegranate.

Turning in the seat to let me slip by, she advises, "Share it with your wife."

"I will, and thank you," I call over my shoulder. Once again standing in the snow, feeling the plump fruit in my coat pocket, I watch the bus drag its squares of yellow light into the darkness. I wave, but in the fogged windows I can see no one waving back.

The snow in our lane crunches with the dryness of sand. It has stayed cold more days than I can recall. I have been trapped in this state of *déjà vu* more minutes than I can recall. Walking home, occasionally I sense the puppet strings relaxing, but as soon as I try to move in any direction except the one ordained for me, the strings jerk taut and I am driven forward. My own dogs, prowling in the circle of illumination beneath the barn light, bark at me as at a stranger. Only my voice reassures them. They broom the snow with their tails as they prance around me on my way to the door.

The knob turns without my key, and I am angry with Sharon for leaving the door unlocked again. But that is not what I must talk

with her about. So when she looks up with a caredrawn face from
the kitchen table, I say to her, "I'm supposed to crawl into your arms
and never come out."

She returns me a strained smile. "What did the doctor say?"

"The ankle's fine. I'm fit for war."

"They won't get you, Gordon. I've sat here all day thinking of
ways to fool them." Folding a sheet of paper which lay on the table
beside her, she seems to catch herself on the verge of reading me
her list of schemes. "But that can wait until tomorrow. Now you
must eat."

"I'm not hungry."

"But you've had nothing since lunch."

"Sweetheart, please, I don't want to eat. I want to talk." Peeling
the coat from my shoulders, I remember the fruit in my pocket, and
say, "How do you eat a pomegranate?"

"What on earth made you think of that? We don't have one."

"I do," holding it in my hand for her to see. "A woman on the
bus gave it to me."

For Sharon, a giving person, this gift is no mystery. So she cuts
it open, spoons the nested seeds from inside, and together we stain
our lips scarlet with the juice as we talk across the kitchen table.

After explaining to her my day's experiences, I conclude: "And
so everything seems to have happened before, as if it were stored
on film and the film were being replayed."

"Even what you're telling me right now?"

"Even now. I feel as if every moment is laid out ahead of time.
I see myself leaning on this table with my elbows, I watch the smear
of juice on your lips, I hear our voices — and it's all like an old film."

"Well, just do something crazy. Get up and dance. Do anything
to snap the illusion."

"I can't. I've tried that all day. But every time I think I'm about
to do something really free, I realize that whatever I do has been
lying there in my future, waiting for me."

Although she faces me across the table, her chestnut eyes do not
look straight into mine. All day other people have focused their gaze
a few degrees away from where I think I am, as if I really were split
in two, and my ghostly second self were drawing their attention.

"It's paranoia," she says. "You have to see that. It's illusion. For weeks you've been talking about feeling trapped in the huge machine that runs this country . . ."

". . . and runs the army, and as much of the world as possible."

"Yes, yes." Her eyes shift their warm stare, but they never quite seem to fix on me. "The machine. The system. You've been brooding about it so long, you've persuaded yourself it's taken you over completely. That's where the puppet feeling comes from."

Now I understand that faint ache of understanding which has pressed on the edges of my mind several times during the day. "And what if they really have taken me over?"

"Rubbish. You're talking nonsense." I can hear the margin of fear in her voice, and I realize that it is fear of me, fear of this obsessed creature I am becoming. But I am powerless to resist the words speaking through me.

"No," shaking my head, "it's not paranoia. Not illusion. I've lived through these minutes before. I've lived through this whole day before." Now the leaps of mind frighten me. "In fact, maybe I've never lived any other day but this one. Maybe all my memories of past days are only part of the old delusion that I'm breaking out of."

"Gordon, please —"

"So today for the first time I'm seeing through the illusion that traps everyone else — the illusion of freedom, of days unrolling, of the future. Maybe we're all caught in this one day, forced to go through it forever. And every night sleep erases our knowledge of this time, only leaves us memories of the illusory yesterdays. But for some reason or other, I've broken through. I *know* I've lived this day before."

Sharon watches me with that cautious alarm I've seen her show toward drunken tramps in bus stations. I can feel her mind resisting the temptation of turning me into a clinical case. When she speaks, her voice betrays an inner struggle for calmness. "Now let's think about this. You've been under strain because of the army . . . because of the war. There's jail to worry about."

"It's not paranoia." I can hear the agitation, verging on frenzy, in my own voice. Yet I feel aloof from my words, as if they were crying at me from a tape recorder.

"Then maybe it's just exhaustion. Tricks of your nerves. You could imagine yourself trapped in today, couldn't you, if it was the only way of keeping tomorrow from coming? The only way of keeping out of jail or out of war?"

"I *know* this day, every minute of it!" I cry, slamming the table, scattering pomegranate seeds. The rage which shakes my voice and drives me lurching toward the door seems remote from my innermost self, which is hiding again in the catacomb of my mind.

"Gordon—let's go sleep."

"You want me to forget."

"No, no, my darling. You must rest. You've got to clear your mind."

"You *do* want me to forget. You want me to slip back into the old delusion that every day is a new one." Against my will I find myself stuffing arms into my coat, drawing laces tight on my boots.

"You're not going out?" she demands in a startled voice.

"I have to walk. To think." Walls are rising in my mind, shutting me off from this woman I love.

"But it's freezing out. It's so late." Invisible wires tug me to the door, even though some voice deep inside me screams *stay, stay.* "You don't even have your hat on, or your gloves." My wired hands pull the door open. "Gordon, don't go away from me. Please don't go away." Her voice bores through all barriers to reach me, like a termite in the woody pulp of my brain. For a second I balance on the threshold, all my love and desire drawing me back into the kitchen, all the force of this tyrannical day dragging me outside into the darkness.

The puppetmaster wins, and I am yanked through the door into falling snow. Air seeps into my lungs like needles. My boots make no sound in the white fluff that blankets everything. No matter which way I turn in my walking, knowledge of the next few seconds seizes me. By the time I reach the highway, where traffic has nearly ceased for the night, I have split in two again. With one self I watch the other scuff boots on a ditchbank, roll a ball of snow, scrape a wad of pitch from a jack pine. I can no longer think clearly, because my mind is so filled with this foreknowledge. But I struggle to hold onto Sharon's words: *Do something crazy. Get up and dance. Do any-*

thing to snap the illusion. I replay them in my mind obsessively, like a mantra, because there is a hint in them of escape.

A splash of yellow light on the roadside jerks my head up, and I see a snowplow bearing down on me. Although its weight shudders the ground, it is uncannily silent, as if it charges at me out of a silent film. I wait on the heaped ridge of snow at the road's brim for it to pass. But Sharon's words echo in me, *do anything to snap the illusion,* and I feel an impulse to leap in front of the truck's blade. Then will I be free of this day? It nears, it nears, flashing its yellow lights, violent as an avalanche, and I have to choose within a second between these two impulses, to stay or to leap.

I am frozen in place at the roadside, not because I have chosen to live, but because whatever power is living me has refused to let me move. The snowplow rumbles past.

Bed draws me with a gravity I cannot resist. In it I will find Sharon awake, her chestnut eyes staring open. Sleep sucks me homeward with promises of forgetting, of breaking open tomorrow a new day.

I awake from feverish sleep to the thunder of jets overhead, which reminds me that I must go this morning for x-rays at the airbase. The daylight world knifes into me.

Acknowledgments

At various times during the writing of these stories I lived on the grace of other people's generosity. I am deeply thankful for the support I have received from the Danforth Foundation, the Marshall Aid Commemoration Commission, the Phillips Exeter Academy, Indiana University, and the National Endowment for the Arts. Although I list the names of institutions, I am mindful of the many people who stand behind the labels, and those are the ones I thank.

ILLINOIS SHORT FICTION

Crossings by Stephen Minot
A Season for Unnatural Causes by Philip F. O'Connor
Curving Road by John Stewart
Such Waltzing Was Not Easy by Gordon Weaver

Rolling All the Time by James Ballard
Love in the Winter by Daniel Curley
To Byzantium by Andrew Fetler
Small Moments by Nancy Huddleston Packer

One More River by Lester Goldberg
The Tennis Player by Kent Nelson
A Horse of Another Color by Carolyn Osborn
The Pleasures of Manhood by Robley Wilson, Jr.

The New World by Russell Banks
The Actes and Monuments by John William Corrington
Virginia Reels by William Hoffman
Up Where I Used to Live by Max Schott

The Return of Service by Jonathan Baumbach
On the Edge of the Desert by Gladys Swan
Surviving Adverse Seasons by Barry Targan
The Gasoline Wars by Jean Thompson

Desirable Aliens by John Bovey
Naming Things by H. E. Francis
Transports and Disgraces by Robert Henson
The Calling by Mary Gray Hughes

Into the Wind by Robert Henderson
Breaking and Entering by Peter Makuck
The Four Corners of the House by Abraham Rothberg
Ladies Who Knit for a Living by Anthony E. Stockanes

Pastorale by Susan Engberg
Home Fires by David Long
The Canyons of Grace by Levi Peterson
Babaru by B. Wongar

Bodies of the Rich by John J. Clayton
Music Lesson by Martha Lacy Hall
Fetching the Dead by Scott R. Sanders
Some of the Things I Did Not Do by Janet Beeler Shaw